# Risking it all to save his friends

"I-I have to stay," he said.

"Then you're already mad," retorted Periphas. "I thought you were desperate to reach Messenia and find your sister!"

"I am, but . . . The gods didn't send us to Messenia. They sent us here. To Keftiu."

"Look around you, Hylas! Your friends won't have survived this!"

"But if they did—"

"A girl and a lion cub? There's no one here but the dead! If you stay, you'll become one of them!"

Hylas licked his lips. "Pirra and Havoc are my friends. I sent them here. I can't abandon them."

"What about us? Aren't we your friends?"

"They need me, Periphas," said Hylas. "It's my *fault* that they're here. If there's a chance they're still alive . . ."

Soon afterward, Hylas was watching the ship heading out over the gray Sea. He watched till it was gone, and he was left alone with the vultures and the icy wind: a stranger in a haunted land ravaged by Plague.

*What have I done?* he wondered.

# Other Books You May Enjoy

GODS AND WARRIORS

THE
EYE OF THE
FALCON

# GODS AND WARRIORS

## THE EYE OF THE FALCON

### MICHELLE PAVER

BOOK

3

PUFFIN BOOKS

PUFFIN BOOKS
An imprint of Penguin Random House LLC
375 Hudson Street
New York, New York 10014

First published in the United States of America by Dial Books for Young Readers,
an imprint of Penguin Young Readers Group, 2015
Published in Great Britain by Penguin Books Ltd, 2014
Published by Puffin Books, an imprint of Penguin Random House LLC, 2016

Text copyright © 2014 by Michelle Paver
Maps, logo, and illustrations copyright © 2013 by Puffin Books
Maps and illustrations by Fred van Deelen
Logo design by James Fraser

THE LIBRARY OF CONGRESS HAS CATALOGED
THE DIAL BOOKS FOR YOUNG READERS EDITION AS FOLLOWS:
Paver, Michelle.
Eye of the falcon / by Michelle Paver.
pages cm.—(Gods and warriors ; [3])
Summary: "Hylas and Pirra travel to the House of the Goddess in hopes of finding the proph-
esized dagger, only to find themselves battling the Crows in a fight to save Pirra's homeland
from destruction"—Provided by publisher.
ISBN: 978-0-8037-3881-2 (hardcover)
[1. Voyages and travels—Fiction. 2. Prehistoric peoples—Fiction.
3. Human-animal communication—Fiction. 4. Gods—Fiction. 5. Bronze age—Fiction.
6. Mediterranean Region—History—To 476—Fiction.]
I. Title.
PZ7.P2853Eye 2015   [Fic]—dc23   2014014515

Puffin Books ISBN 978-0-14-242302-8

Designed by Nancy R. Leo-Kelly

Printed in the United States of America

1 3 5 7 9 10 8 6 4 2

# THE WORLD OF GODS AND WARRIORS

# 1

"What *happened* here?" said Hylas. "Where are all the people?"

"There's one over there," said Periphas, "but he's not going to tell us." He pointed at a ship that the Sea had flung halfway up a hill. Snagged in its rigging was the skeleton of a man. Shreds of rotten tunic flapped in the wind, and one bony arm swung in a grisly wave.

"Looks like the gods punished Keftiu worst of all," said Glaukos.

"Smells like it too," said Medon. The others muttered and gripped their amulets.

Hylas was stunned. Over the winter he'd seen many horrors, but nothing like this. The Sea had smashed huts, boats, trees, animals, people. The shore was eerily silent, and wherever he turned, he saw mounds of rotting wreckage. Dirty gray surf clawed at his boots, and he breathed the throat-catching stink of death. How could Pirra and Havoc have survived this?

With his knife, Periphas turned over the skull of an ox. "This happened months ago. Everything's covered in ash."

"But someone must've survived," said Hylas. "Why didn't they come back and rebuild?"

No one answered.

"This *can't* be Keftiu," said Hylas. "It's a huge rich island with thousands of people, Pirra told me!"

"I'm sorry, lad," said Periphas. "You won't find your friends now. We'll see if there's anything worth taking, then we're off."

While the others spread out to forage, Hylas spotted a hut farther down the shore and picked his way toward it, desperate to find someone alive.

The icy wind tugged at his sheepskins, and he startled a vulture, which flew off, raising a haze of ash. He hardly noticed. All through the winter the Great Cloud had hidden the Sun, plunging the world into perpetual twilight and shrouding it in ash. He'd grown used to the gloom, and the black grit that got into hair, clothes, food. But *this . . .*

He thought of his friends as he'd last seen them, seven moons ago on Thalakrea. The Mountain had been spewing fire and there'd been chaos on the shore, people fleeing in whatever boats they could find. Somehow, he'd gotten Havoc and Pirra on a ship: Havoc scrabbling in her cage and yowling at him, *Why are you abandoning me,* and Pirra white with fury—for the ship was Keftian. "I *told* you I couldn't go back!" she'd screamed. "I'll never forgive you, Hylas! I'll hate you forever!"

He'd done it to *save* her. But he'd sent her to this.

The hut was mud-brick and thatch, and someone had crudely repaired it after the Sea's attack. They'd also marked the wall with a stark white handprint. Hylas didn't know what that meant, but it felt like a warning. He halted some distance away.

The wind flung more ash in his face. As he brushed it off, he felt an ache in his temple, and from the corner of his eye, he glimpsed two ragged children. They vanished inside, but he saw that they were girls, one about ten, the other younger. Both had bizarrely shaven heads, except for one long lock hanging from the temple, and angry boils on their necks the size of pigeons' eggs.

"I'm not going to hurt you!" he called.

No answer, but he knew they were listening. And he caught a sense of anger, and hopeless searching.

To reassure them, he turned his back.

Again they appeared at the corner of his vision.

"Are you looking for your parents?" he said without moving his head. "I'm looking for someone too. My friends. Is anyone else alive?"

Still no answer. The anger and loss came at him in waves.

Belatedly, he remembered that he was a foreigner here, so they wouldn't understand him. "I'm Akean," he explained. "I can't speak Keftian!"

Once again when he looked, they vanished inside. After a moment's hesitation, he followed.

The hut was empty.

Yes, empty—and no way out except for this door. The back of his neck began to prickle, and his hand went to the lion-claw amulet at his throat.

Dim gray light filtered through the thatch, and the air was thick with the stench of death. Then on a cot against the opposite wall, he saw the bodies of two girls.

His heart hammered against his ribs.

One girl looked about ten, the other younger. Both had shaven heads with a single lock of hair at the temple, and terrible boils on their necks. A dark haze seemed to boil and swarm around them, like ash—only this was alive.

With a cry Hylas staggered from the hut.

Farther up the shore, the others were already splashing through the shallows to the ship, and Periphas was hastily untying its line from a boulder. "Where've you been!" he yelled at Hylas. "We're clearing out, we found bodies!"

"So did I!" gasped Hylas.

"Did you touch them?" barked Periphas.

"No, I—no." He didn't dare mention the children. His mind shied away from what they might be.

No one sees ghosts, he told himself. And yet I saw them. They were there.

"We found three fresh corpses in a shelter," muttered Periphas. "Black in the face, and all over with boils."

"What *is* it?" said Hylas.

"Plague," snapped Periphas.

The men within earshot blanched.

Hylas' mind reeled. "M-maybe it's only on this part of the coast," he stammered. "If we go farther—"

"I'm not risking it," said Periphas.

"Then inland! There are mountains, we can—"

"Let me tell you about the Plague," Periphas cut in. "It comes with the unburied dead. That's what happened here. First you get a fever. That's the Plague making its nests in your flesh. Soon those nests swell into great agonizing boils. They hurt so much you can't stop screaming, but the Plague doesn't care, it's breeding inside you. Now the boils are bursting, and the pain's so bad you're going mad." He chucked the line toward the ship. "It only ends one way."

The others had stopped what they were doing and were gaping at their leader.

Hylas glanced from Periphas to the ruined shore and the hazy mountains beyond. "I-I have to stay," he said.

"Then you're already mad," retorted Periphas. "I thought you were desperate to reach Messenia and find your sister!"

"I am, but . . . The gods didn't send us to Messenia. They sent us here. To Keftiu."

"Look around you, Hylas! Your friends won't have survived this!"

"But if they did—"

"A girl and a lion cub? There's no one here but the dead! If you stay, you'll become one of them!"

Hylas licked his lips. "Pirra and Havoc are my friends. I sent them here. I can't abandon them."

"What about us? Aren't we your friends?"

Hylas glanced at the others on the ship. They were tough men—escaped slaves like him—and used to unimaginable hardship. At nearly fourteen, he was the youngest by far, and yet they'd treated him with rough kindness. For seven moons they'd been trying to get back to Akea, but the Sea was full of huge floating islands of pumice, and they kept losing their way. Once, they'd run aground; it had taken two moons to repair the ship. And now they'd fetched up here, on Keftiu.

Hylas looked at Periphas, with his broken nose and his brown eyes that had seen too many bad things. Periphas had saved his life by hauling him aboard as the ship left Thalakrea. He'd been a warrior once, and over the winter he'd taught Hylas a bit about fighting. In a way, they'd become friends.

But Pirra was different—and so was Havoc.

"They need me, Periphas," said Hylas. "It's *my fault* that they're here. If there's a chance they're still alive . . ."

Periphas gave him a strange, angry look. Then he scratched his beard with one grimy hand. "It's your choice," he growled. "A pity. I liked you."

After that, things happened fast. Hylas already carried his axe, knife, slingshot, and strike-fire, but now Periphas gave him a waterskin, a sack of provisions, and a coil of rope. "That always comes in handy," he said with a scowl.

Soon afterward, Hylas was watching the ship heading

out over the gray Sea. He watched till it was gone, and he was left alone with the vultures and the icy wind: a stranger in a haunted land ravaged by Plague.

*What have I done?* he wondered.

Then he hoisted his gear on his back and headed off to find his friends.

# 2

Hylas could see snow on the mountains, and here on the coast the wind was freezing, but the cold didn't bother the lumpy little creature squatting in front of him. It was about knee height and made of dirty wax, with hair of moldy straw and fierce red pebble eyes.

Periphas had warned him about these as he was leaving. "They're Plague traps, they draw it away from the living. People call them pus-eaters. Make sure you don't touch."

As Hylas edged past the pus-eater, he felt an ache in his temple, and rubbed the scar from the burn he'd received on Thalakrea. The ache faded, but from the corner of his eye, he glimpsed dark specks crawling all over the pus-eater. He'd seen the same black swarm on the ghostly children. Was it Plague? Periphas hadn't said anything about being able to *see* it, so how could this be?

And how was it possible that he was seeing ghosts?

There was no one to ask. He hadn't met anyone all day, either living or dead. To his right, the gray Sea sucked at the shore, and to his left, low gray hills barred the way inland. Halfway up, a dark band of wreckage was a grim reminder of the Sea's attack.

Periphas had told him that if he followed the coast west for a day or so, then headed inland, he would reach the House of the Goddess, where Pirra's mother ruled. "Although who knows what you'll find. There used to be villages and ship-sheds all along this coast. Where we're standing used to be a town."

"What's a town?" Hylas had asked.

"Like a village, but bigger. Thousands of people."

*"Thousands?"*

"Keftiu is vast, Hylas, it takes two days to sail from one end to the other. Even if your friends are still alive, how will you find them?"

That had only been this morning, but already Periphas seemed long gone. Hylas felt lonely, vulnerable, and *cold*. He wished he had something warmer than a sheepskin jerkin whose sleeves were too short, and leggings with holes in the knees.

Up ahead, he saw smoke rising from behind a spur. Drawing his knife, he crept forward and peered around a boulder.

He blinked in disbelief.

Below him at the head of a bay clustered several make-shift huts with people bustling about in between, oblivious to the desolation. Some stirred huge steaming cauldrons; others bent over stone vats cut into the hillside, or unloaded dripping baskets from boats in the shallows. Even more bizarre, women stood at drying racks, hanging up sodden armfuls of astonishing colored wool. Scarlet, yellow, blue, purple: The brilliant clots of color seemed to throb in the grayness all around.

The wind gusted in Hylas' face, and he inhaled an eye-watering stench of urine and rotting fish. In astonishment, he realized that these people must be dye-workers. But why would anyone bother to dye wool in a Plague?

He was debating whether to go down and seek shelter or avoid them altogether, when a stone struck the boulder near his head. He spun around—guessed it was a trick—flung himself sideways. Too late. A noose yanked tight around his neck, his knife was kicked from his hand, and spears pinned him front and back.

---

"I *told* you, I'm not a thief!" shouted Hylas.

His captors yelled at him in Keftian, brandishing fishing spears and big double axes of tarnished bronze. There were ten of them: squat beardless men in ragged sheepskin tunics baring muscular limbs stained a weird, blotchy purple. Their faces were purple too, and they stank of urine and rotting fish. Hylas had never seen anything like them.

One man hooked Hylas' axe from his belt, then they hauled and pushed him down to the huts, keeping him at a distance with their spears, for fear of Plague.

Still yelling in their strange bird-like speech, they halted at the largest hut, and an old woman appeared in the doorway: Hylas guessed she was the headwoman of the village.

She was enormously fat, and swathed in layers of filthy gray rags. She had a spongy purple face crowned with a few greasy threads of hair. One eye socket was empty, the other eye was a cloudy gray. It skittered about alarmingly, then fastened on Hylas and gave him a hard stare.

One of the men pointed to the tattoo on Hylas' forearm: the black zigzag that marked him as a slave of the Crows. Over the winter, he'd tattooed a line underneath, to turn it into a longbow. That didn't seem to fool the old woman.

"What's a Crow spy doing here?" she rasped in Akean.

"I'm not a Crow," panted Hylas, "and I'm not a spy, I—"

"We drown Crow spies. We feed them to the sea snails."

"I *hate* the Crows! I'm just trying to find my friend! Her name's Pirra, she's the daughter of High Priestess Yassassara."

The woman snorted. "As if she'd be friends with the likes of you." Barking a command in Keftian, she jerked her head, and the men began to drag Hylas toward the Sea.

"I can prove it!" he shouted. "Pirra grew up in the House of the Goddess, she told me it's huge and—they do rites with men jumping over charging bulls—"

"Everyone knows that," sneered the woman.

They were hauling him over stinking mounds of crushed sea snails, past conical baskets baited with rotting fish. Was that how he was going to end up? As bait?

"Pirra hated the House of the Goddess," he shouted over his shoulder, "she called it her stone prison! Then her mother tried to strike a bargain with the Crows, she was going to seal it by giving Pirra in marriage—but Pirra burned her own face to spoil the match! She—she's got a scar like a crescent moon on her cheek—"

"Everyone knows that too," called the woman.

"You can't *do* this!" he yelled. "I'm a stranger here, it's against the law of the gods to kill a stranger!"

"The gods have abandoned Keftiu," snarled the woman. "Around here, *I* make the law!"

Now they were dragging him into the freezing shallows and kicking him to his knees. Icy waves stung his face. The tines of a pitchfork enclosed his neck, forcing him toward the water . . .

Something Pirra had said came back to him. "She had a tunic of Keftian purple!" he blurted out. "She said they make the purple from mashed-up sea snails, thousands of them, and it costs more than gold!"

The woman barked a command, and the pressure on his neck lifted. Panting, he lurched to his feet.

"Quite a few people know that too," the woman called drily. "You'll have to do better if you want to live."

"She—um—once she told me there were only two robes like it in all Keftiu," he gasped, "but nobody's ever seen the other because it's Yassassara's, they made it in secret, she only wears it for secret rites."

Silence. The gray Sea lapped hungrily at his thighs.

"I dyed that wool myself," said the woman. "By moon-light. In secret. Now, how'd you know that?"

"Like I said, Pirra told me!"

Another command—and Hylas was hauled back to the shore. The noose was removed, the spears withdrawn. Someone chucked him his axe and his knife.

The old woman hawked and spat a gobbet of purple snot on the stones. Then she turned and lumbered back into her hut. "Yassassara's dead," she said over her shoulder.

Hylas flinched. "What about Pirra?"

"You better come inside."

# 3

The lion cub heard ravens calling from the ridge and quickened her pace. Ravens meant carcasses, and she was hungry.

The Bright Soft Cold lay deep on the mountain, and by the time she'd struggled onto the ridge, the ravens had left only bones. The cub crunched them up, but the hunger didn't go away.

The cub was always hungry. Long ago, men had brought her to this horrible land of shadows and ghosts. She remembered fleeing in terror as the Great Gray Beast came roaring in and savaged the shore. Afterward, there had been piles of carcasses—dogs, sheep, goats, fish, humans—and swarms of vultures. The lion cub had fought for her share, until men had chased her away with their great shiny claws.

She'd fled to the mountain, because she *knew* mountains, but this was nothing like the fiery Mountain where she'd lived with her pride. *There were no lions,* only frozen trees and Bright Soft Cold; hungry creatures, ragged men, and ghosts.

It was a land of shadows. When the cub sat on her

haunches and gazed at the Up, she couldn't see the Great Lion whose mane shone golden in the Light and silver in the Dark. And there was no real Light, only this gray not-Light, in between the Darks.

The cub had grown used to the not-Light, as it helped her hide from men; but as the Darks and the not-Lights passed, the cold bit harder. Her breath turned to smoke, and she couldn't find any wet to drink, so she ate the Bright Soft Cold. She learned to crawl into caves when the white wind howled, and her pelt grew thick and matted with filth. It kept her warm, but she was too hungry and frightened to lick herself clean.

Then, alarmingly, her teeth started falling out. She was horrified, until new ones thrust painfully through. They were larger and stronger than the old ones: She could rip open a frozen carcass with one bite. And she got bigger. Now when she stood on her hind legs to scratch a tree, her forepaws reached much higher than before.

Here on the mountain, there weren't as many dead things as on the shore, so as well as scavenging, the cub tried to hunt. Mostly she did it wrong, charging too soon, or getting confused about which prey to chase; but *finally* she felled a squirrel with a lucky swipe. It was her first kill. If only there'd been someone with her, to see.

That was the worst of it, the loneliness. Sometimes the cub sat and mewed her misery to the Up. She longed for warmth and muzzle-rubs—and to sleep without fear, because other ears and noses were keeping watch.

A jay cawed to its mate, and from high on the ridge came the squawks of vultures. The lion cub struggled toward them through the Bright Soft Cold.

The vultures were squabbling over a dead roebuck. The cub wasn't yet able to roar, so she rushed at them, snarling as loud as she could and lashing out with her claws. It was good to see the vultures flying off in a clatter of wings; and the buck was still warm. Tearing open its belly, the cub hunkered down to feed.

She'd hardly gulped a mouthful when two men burst from the trees, shouting and waving big shiny claws.

The cub fled: down a gully and up some rocks, *anywhere*, as long as she got away. She didn't stop until she could no longer smell that horrible man-stink.

The lion cub hated and feared all men. It was *men*, with their terrible flapping hides and their savage dogs, who had killed her mother and father when she was little. It was *men* who had brought her across the Great Gray Beast to this freezing land of ghosts.

It hadn't always been like this. Long ago when she was small, there had been a boy. She'd had a thorn in her pad, and he'd pulled it out with his thin clever forepaws, then smeared on some healing mud. The boy had looked after the cub and given her meat. She remembered his calm strong voice, and the warmth of his smooth, furless flanks. She remembered his ridiculously long sleeps, and how cross he would get when she jumped on his chest to wake him.

There'd been a girl too. She'd been kind to the cub (except when the cub struck at her ankles to trip her up). For a few Lights and Darks, they'd been a pride together: boy, girl, and cub. They'd been happy. The cub remembered uproarious games of play-hunt, and the humans' yelping laughs when she pounced. She remembered a magic ball of sticks that could fly without wings, and race downhill without any legs. She remembered much meat and muzzle-rubbing and warmth . . .

A clump of Bright Soft Cold slid off a branch and spattered the cub. Wearily, she shook it off.

It hurt to remember the boy, because he was the one who had sent her here to this horrible place. He had abandoned her.

The lion cub snuffed the air, then plodded on between the cold unfeeling trees.

She would never trust another human. Not ever again.

# 4

"You speak Akean," ventured Hylas as he stood shivering in the gloom.

"Well of course I do," snapped the one-eyed old woman, "I *am* Akean. Name's Gorgo. What's yours?"

"Flea," lied Hylas.

"Your real one."

". . . Hylas."

Gorgo subsided onto a bench before a large fire and arranged her vast belly over her knees. An elderly sheephound heaved himself to his feet and limped over to her, swinging his tail. From a pail, she sloshed milk into a potsherd and watched the dog lap it up. "You just going to stand there?" she barked.

It took Hylas a moment to realize she was speaking to him.

"Feed the fire, then sit," she commanded. "I can see you've not got the Plague, but if you don't dry off, you'll die anyway."

Hylas fed the fire with dried cowpats, then poured seawater out of his boots and huddled as close to the fire as he could without getting scorched. The hut was dark and cramped; he tried to ignore the stink of urine and rotten fish.

With a blotchy purple paw, Gorgo scratched the bristles on her chin. Her cloudy gray eye veered all over the hut, then skewered Hylas. "So. You were a slave of the Crows."

He nodded. "In the mines of Thalakrea."

Gorgo grunted. "I hear that's where it started. The Crows dug too deep and angered the gods. Because of the Crows, the Sun's gone, we've had the coldest winter anyone can remember, and there is no spring."

Hylas bit back the urge to ask about Pirra. He sensed that the old woman would tell him when she was ready, not before. "What happened here?" he said, his teeth chattering with cold. "I'm a stranger on Keftiu, I—"

"Then your luck just ran out," said Gorgo. Jabbing her knuckle in her empty eye socket, she gave it a vigorous scratch. "First we knew, the Great Cloud was blotting out the Sun and the ash was raining down. Then the Great Wave." She scowled. "They say some people just stood and stared. Others fled. Wave got them all. Faster than a horse can gallop. Didn't see it myself. We'd taken a load of wool inland to be weighed. Bit of luck, or we'd of drowned."

With a stick, she stabbed the fire. "My sons say they never smelled anything like the stink of the bodies, but I wouldn't know." A juddering laugh shook her mountainous flesh. "I can't smell. Never have." She spat, narrowly missing the dog. "Since that first fall of ash we've had many more. Then the Plague came about a moon ago. It struck the heart of Keftiu. Yassassara ordered everyone out of the House of the Goddess and for all around as far as a man can ride in a day. Villages, farms, emptied. She sent them to the settlements in the west. They can't come back till the priests say the Plague's gone."

Hylas swallowed. "I'm trying to find the House of the Goddess."

"Didn't you hear what I said? There's no point, it's deserted! The High Priestess was going to do a Mystery, get rid of the Plague and bring back the Sun. Ha!" Another juddering laugh. "Plague got her instead."

Hylas was appalled. He'd only seen Yassassara once, but she'd radiated power like heat from embers. How could she have succumbed to Plague?

"Didn't expect that, did you?" Gorgo said drily. "Nobody did. Not even her. They say she had herself carried to her tomb when she was still alive. Had her priests purify the House of the Goddess with sulfur, then seal it up. So now it's empty. Rest of Keftiu's not doing much better. Great Wave got most people on the coast, Plague got half the rest. Priests have been busy, sacrificing rams, bulls, but nothing's worked. Survivors still holed up in the west, a few hiding out in the mountains." She sniffed. "And with no one to bury the bodies, we've got all these ghosts wandering about. They're *angry*, no proper rites, no one to put them at rest in the tombs of their kin."

Hylas went still. "Can you—see them?"

She glared at him. "Course not! Why'd you think that?"

He ducked the question. "Aren't you afraid of the Plague? I mean, why are you still here?"

Again her bloated body shook with laughter. "We smell so bad, not even *Plague* comes near us! Nobody comes near dye-workers, we've always lived apart. And now with all this rotten meat in the Sea, why *wouldn't* we stay? It's the best sea snail harvest we've ever had! Plenty of wool about too, all those lost sheep wandering around for the taking." She slapped her belly. "That's why I'm so fat!"

"But who's going to buy your wool?"

"Look," snapped Gorgo. "If the Sun never comes back, the crops fail and we all die. If the Sun does come back, things'll get better and we'll be rich. Either way, we keep working."

Hylas held his hands over the fire and watched his tunic steam. "Why was Keftiu hit harder than anywhere else?"

"*Because of Yassassara!*" roared Gorgo, causing the dog to set back his ears, and one of her sons to put his head in the door.

Hylas sat very still and waited for Gorgo to calm down.

"You said it yourself," she growled, waving her son away. "Yassassara tried to bargain with the Crows. So when the gods punished them by blowing up Thalakrea, they punished us too. Oh, she *knew* it was her fault. That's why she was going to do the Mystery, to make up for it."

Hylas mustered his courage. "So where's Pirra?"

Gorgo's eye became opaque, like that of a snake before it sheds its skin. Hylas had a sudden sense that she knew a lot more than she was letting on. "How should I know?" she said. "Now suppose *you* stop asking questions, and tell *me* what an Outsider from Lykonia is doing on Keftiu."

Hylas tensed. "What makes you think I'm an Outsider?"

For a heartbeat, she hesitated. "They're the only people I know with yellow hair."

He wondered how much to reveal. "I was a goatherd. The Crows attacked my camp and killed my dog. I got separated from my little sister. That was"—he caught his breath—"nearly two years ago."

Gorgo narrowed her eye. "Why'd they attack you?"

"I don't know." But he did. The Crows wanted him dead because an Oracle had foretold that if an Outsider wielded their ancestral dagger—the dagger of Koronos—it would be their ruin. But he wasn't about to tell a stranger that.

"What's your sister's name?" Gorgo said abruptly.

"What?—Issi."

Again she scratched her bristly chin. "Did you find her?"

"No. I think she's in Messenia. If—if she's still alive."

"Messenia." Gorgo's eye turned inward, remembering. "Long time since I heard that name." The dog put his muzzle on her knee, but she ignored him. "Dark soon," she said abruptly to the fire. "You got till nightfall to get out of arrowshot of my village. Don't ever come back."

Hylas blinked. "You mean—you're letting me go?"

Reaching under the bench, she pulled out a small wovengrass pouch and chucked it at him. "Fleabane and sulfur. Might keep off the Plague for a bit."

"Thanks," faltered Hylas.

Gorgo glared at him. "Don't you dare *thank* me!" she bellowed. "Get out and never come back!"

Hylas was leaving the village at a run, when she shouted after him: "That daughter of Yassassara's! I hear they took her to the mountains—to Taka Zimi! But that was moons ago, just after the Great Wave, and they say there's Plague up that way, and some monster stalking the forest—she'll be dead by now!"

# 5

Pirra is on the deck of the ship, screaming at Hylas. "I hate you! I'll *hate* you for*ever*!" She goes on screaming as the ship pulls away and he is lost from sight.

Now the voyage is over, the ship has reached Keftiu, and Pirra is watching the sailors unload Havoc's cage. The lion cub is frightened and miserable. She's been seasick all the way, and has rubbed her forehead raw on the bars, but Pirra couldn't let her out in case she jumped overboard.

They're hardly ashore when something terrible happens: The Sea begins to withdraw. Pirra stares in disbelief at glistening mounds of seaweed and stranded, flapping fish. Then the captain remembers a story of the old times and bellows a warning. "It's going to attack! To the hills! *Run!*"

Now the sailors are fleeing in panic and Userref is dragging Pirra up a cliff. She sees Havoc in her cage, abandoned on the rocks, and screams at the men to set the cub free, but Userref won't let go of her wrist and the Great Wave is roaring toward them with vast white claws . . .

Pirra woke up.

She was in bed at Taka Zimi. Her chamber was warm: Embers crackled in the brazier, and she lay in a nest of sheepskins. She smelled the wormwood that Userref burned to ward off the Plague, and heard the distant roar of the waterfall and the gurgle of water collecting in the cistern under the sanctuary. But the dream clung to her. She remembered the terrible silence after the Great Wave had gone.

She shut her eyes. She hadn't actually *seen* Havoc washed away. Maybe someone *had* let the cub out, and she'd escaped in time . . .

Round and round Pirra's thoughts circled: from grief for Havoc, to shock and disbelief over her mother, to rage and anxiety—mostly rage—about Hylas.

As her heartbeats slowed, she realized she was clutching her amulet pouch, which held the falcon feather he'd given her two summers before. Falcons are creatures of the Goddess, but Pirra loved them simply because they enjoyed a freedom she didn't have. It had meant a lot when Hylas had given her this feather.

But things were different now. All through the winter she'd had fights with him in her head. "I told you I'd die if I was sent back to Keftiu—and yet you did it anyway!"

"I was saving your life," replied the Hylas in her head.

"You should've left that to *me*! If you hadn't forced me onto the ship, I'd have found another—probably the same one as you—and I'd be *free*! Instead I'm shut up here forever, and it's all your fault!"

"And me?" said the imaginary Hylas. "What if I drowned in the Great Wave, and you're arguing with a ghost?"

And so it went on.

Suddenly, Pirra couldn't take it anymore. Yanking open the pouch, she pulled out the small tattered feather. She'd kept it through fire and flood. Well, not anymore. She had to get Hylas out of her head.

Swiftly, she drew on woolen leggings, a long-sleeved tunic of otter fur, and calfskin boots lined with fleece, then flung on her fox-fur mantle. Ripping a twist of wool from her hair, she found a small stone lamp and tied on Hylas' feather, to weigh it down. Then she slipped quietly out of her chamber.

At the shrine, lamps glimmered before the bronze Watchers who sent their metal prayers to the Goddess while Her human worshippers slept. Pirra put her fist to her forehead and bowed, then crept out onto the steps.

Her spirits plummeted, as they always did when she saw the sky. Though it was night, she couldn't see the Moon or the stars. The Great Cloud shrouded the world. It was like being in a tomb.

The sanctuary of Taka Zimi perched like an eyrie high on a shoulder of Mount Dikti, with its back against the mountainside and a precipice in front. It was a long narrow building split into four: Pirra's chamber at one end, then the shrine, then two chambers for Userref and Pirra's hated slave girl, Silea, with the cellar and cistern beneath.

In front of the sanctuary was a small snowy courtyard

enclosed by massive stone walls twenty cubits high. At the far end of the courtyard, the guards' quarters and the heavy barred gates occupied one corner, while in the other, stone pegs jutting from the wall led up to a windy lookout post, where a shaggy old juniper tree clung to life on the edge of the precipice.

Torches burned between the stone bulls' horns on top of the walls, but the guards' quarters were dark. All Pirra could hear was the thunder of the waterfall and the hiss of windblown snow.

She thought of the endless walks she'd made around the courtyard, and of her pathetic plan of escape. Whenever Silea was busy, she would sneak into the slave girl's room and kick aside the mat that covered the hatch to the cellar. Down there in the freezing dark, she would hack at the wall where the pipe carried water from the stream outside into the cistern in the cellar. Over the winter, she'd managed to dislodge one stone, creating a hole about the size of her fist.

"This is your fault, Hylas," she whispered. "You're why I'm here."

Racing across the courtyard, she climbed the pegs to the lookout. The screaming wind blasted her with snow, and she grabbed the trunk of the juniper tree to steady herself. In her free hand she gripped the lamp with the feather tied on. When she threw it, it would be gone for good.

Somewhere, a crow cawed, and for a moment, Pirra thought of the Crow warriors on Thalakrea. They'd escaped to safety. Had they found out that she'd taken their precious dagger?

Hylas hadn't given her the chance to tell him; he'd been too busy forcing her onto the ship. Well, if he believed the Crows still had the dagger, that only served him right.

"Get out of my head, Hylas," she muttered, and leaned over the precipice as far as she dared.

"Pirra, what are you *doing*?" shouted Userref. He stood on the sanctuary steps, frozen with horror.

"Getting rid of something!" she yelled. Drawing back her arm, she flung the lamp—and the wind tore it away into the whirling void. "There!" she shouted. "That's the last of you gone!"

---

"You *promised* you wouldn't climb up there," admonished Userref when they were back in her chamber and he'd dealt with the guards, who'd been woken by the shouting.

"I didn't *promise*," retorted Pirra.

"Mistress, how *could* you?" scolded Silea. Her plump face puckered with disapproval, although she loved it when Pirra got into trouble.

"Silea, go away," snarled Pirra.

"I wish I could," muttered the slave girl. That was a lie: She was enjoying Taka Zimi, safe from the Plague, and with little to do except flirt with the guards.

"Just *go*," commanded Pirra.

Rolling her eyes, Silea went.

Userref studied Pirra. "What you threw away, was it that falcon feather Hylas gave you?"

Pirra turned on him. "I told you never to speak his name! I *ordered* you! And in case you've forgotten, you're still *my slave,* just like Silea!"

There was a prickly silence. Userref crossed his arms and glowered at the brazier. Pirra snatched up her bronze mirror and glared at herself. The cold made her scar show livid on her cheek. She'd burned her face deliberately when she was twelve, to avoid being wed, but now that she was nearly fourteen, she hated her scar. She'd tried everything to make it fade. Nothing had worked.

Userref looked unhappy. He loathed being angry. Pirra felt a flash of affection for him. He was the big brother she'd never had.

Despite the cold, he still shaved his head in mourning for his beloved Egypt, and painted black stripes across his eyes, in the hopes that it would bring back the Sun. For him even more than for the Keftians, the Sun's disappearance was a catastrophe: He lived by its daily rebirth.

"Sorry," she mumbled.

He gave her a smile that lit up his handsome face. "Doesn't matter, I understand. It's this terrible place."

The frozen mountain had appalled him. "This thing you call *snow,*" he'd exclaimed on their first day at Taka Zimi, "it's everywhere! And some demon has put a spell on my breath and turned it to smoke!"

Pirra had had a struggle to make him wear warm clothes,

as he refused to touch wool, regarding sheep as unclean. At last she'd persuaded him into a linen tunic and leggings padded with goosedown, a harefur cloak, and calfskin boots stuffed with hay.

Pirra noticed that his pouch was slung over his shoulder. "You're going out," she said.

"Down to the village to get more wormwood."

"Let me go with you," she begged.

He sighed. "You know I can't. I swore to your mother."

Pirra blinked. She hated it when he mentioned Yassassara. "The High Priestess is dead," she told him levelly.

"Which makes her wishes sacred."

"For how long? Am I to be shut in here forever?"

"You know the answer. Till the Sun returns and rids the land of Plague."

"What if that never happens?"

"Your mother sent you here to be safe. Now that she's dead, the priests—"

"They don't care about me any more than she did!" Pirra burst out. "They only want me alive so they can trade me in marriage when this is over!"

Userref turned to go, but she ran to him. "Userref, *please!* Let me come with you, even just outside the gates! I won't run away, where would I go? There's nothing but mountains and snow!"

"Pirra—"

"All winter I've been pacing that courtyard! If I do it any more I'll go mad!"

"Pirra I can't! I swore to your mother!"

"My mother is dead dead dead!"

There was a shocked silence. Pirra folded her arms and turned her back on Userref. She had hated her mother, but she'd been stunned by her death, and she was haunted by their last exchange. "You ran away," Yassassara had said coldly. "You shirked your duty to Keftiu."

Pirra had wanted to tell her that on Thalakrea, she'd risked her life for Keftiu—but she'd never gotten the chance. That day she'd been banished to Taka Zimi, and she'd never seen her mother again. Now she couldn't ever make Yassassara proud of her. It was too late.

She turned to find Userref observing her thoughtfully. "You're more like her than you know," he said. "Just as brave and just as strong-willed."

Pirra flinched. Once, Hylas had said something similar. *You're brave and you don't give up.*

With a snarl, she ground her fist against the wall. *Stop* thinking about Hylas.

"And Pirra," said Userref from the doorway. "That feather. It's an emblem of *Heru*, my falcon-headed god. You can't get rid of it as easily as that."

"What do you mean?" Pirra said sulkily.

"You sent it out on the wind. Who knows what the wind will send back?"

# 6

She remembered the Egg. Being all crumpled up inside, with her feet jammed under her beak. She couldn't move a claw, it was awful.

But she *did* move. Twisting her head, she pecked, and panted, and pecked again—and at last the Egg cracked, and she was *free*.

She couldn't see, but she was aware of the other fluffy hatchlings, and of her mother's warm feathers pressing down on her. She smelled droppings, sticks, and rock. She heard her parents' piercing cries, and the roaring air.

She was *hungry*. She jostled and trod on her brothers to get at the meat that her parents stuffed down her beak.

She grew stronger. Now that she could see, she struggled out of the Nest and explored the Ledge. She pulled her brothers' tails with her beak, and peered at the slow, earthbound creatures in the forest far below.

She learned to sharpen her sight by bobbing her head up and down. Soon she could follow three snowflakes at once. She *loved* all the bright colors: a red-and-gold eagle, the brilliant hues of flies. But if a crow flew past, glinting green and purple and black, her talons tightened—because crows steal eggs, and are the enemies of falcons.

After several Lights and Darks, strange itchy bumps began breaking out all over her. She was outraged. Then her fluff fell out and the itchy bumps grew into feathers.

She adored them. They were white, brown, pink, gray, blue; some speckled, all beautifully sleek. She learned to tidy them by running them through her beak with a satisfying *zzzt;* and now when she watched her parents soaring on the Wind, she envied them. She longed to explore the Sky. It was always changing: sometimes dark, sometimes light. During the Lights, the fledgling sensed something vast and powerful hidden behind the clouds. It never showed its face, although she wished it would.

Above all, she longed to fly. She flapped her wings till she was exhausted, but nothing happened.

Then one Light, as she was furiously flapping, the Wind scooped her off the Ledge—and for the flick of a feather, she was very nearly flying!

Abruptly, the Wind dropped her and she fell off the Ledge. She fell for ages, too startled to squawk, and landed in snow. Angry and humiliated, she struggled to her feet and shrieked for her parents, but they'd gone hunting and didn't hear.

The fledgling gaped in terror. She was stuck on the ground like an earthbound creature. She could see the Ledge, horribly high above, but she couldn't get back to it.

She started to crawl over the snow, hoping the Wind

would pick her up again. Instead she slipped and rolled over and over.

She came to rest in a patch of bare earth, by a hole seething with ants. She pecked one. It tasted sour, so she spat it out, but this angered the other ants, and they started biting her feet. So many ants, swarming up her legs and stinging the roots of her feathers. She flapped and shrieked in panic.

The ground shook, and a huge earthbound monster darkened the Sky. He scooped her up and started picking off the ants. His voice was a low rumble, like a distant river; the fledgling found it oddly soothing. *Human,* she thought. *This is a human.*

After picking off the ants, the human placed her in a warm dark nest, which was such a relief that she went to sleep.

She woke in a Windless place with *two* humans: the male who'd saved her from the ants, and a smaller female. Like the male, the girl had neither wings nor beak, but the fledgling was fascinated by her brilliant colors. Instead of feathers, the girl had an odd loose hide that was orange, yellow, and green, with red fur like a fox on her back, and long black hair on her head, streaked purple and blue.

Slowly, the girl reached toward the fledgling, holding a scrap of meat in her big soft talons.

Alarmed, the fledgling rose to her full height, gaping and spreading her wings. Then she snatched the meat in her beak and flung it scornfully aside.

The girl held out more meat. She neither stared nor loomed, she simply spoke in a gentle rumble. Her strange pale face lacked feathers or fluff, but her eyes were as dark as a falcon's, and in them, the fledgling glimpsed a spirit as trapped and flightless as her own.

The fledgling stretched out her neck and took the meat.

———

Pirra watched the fledgling snatch another scrap of mouse in its outsize beak. "Are you *sure* it's a falcon?" she said doubtfully.

Userref's lip curled. "Of course I am."

Pirra snorted. "It's not like any falcon I've ever seen."

The creature huddled in the pouch was a scruffy brown-and-white bundle the size of a pigeon: mostly feathers, except for a few bizarre tufts of white fluff on its head, with lots more on its legs, like fluffy white leggings. It had large yellow-green feet and long black claws, and it was glaring up at Pirra with big, dark, baleful eyes.

"Where'd you find it?" she said.

"On the ground, below a crag. I heard her squawking; she must have fallen out of her nest. It's early in the year for fledglings, but this is such a strange time, the wild creatures don't know if it's winter or spring. This falcon is a good omen. Maybe she'll bring back the Sun."

"How d'you know it's a she?"

"I don't, but I feel it." He paused. "If she lives," he said carefully, "she'll want to fly. Whether or not she does—that's up to you."

"Why?" Pirra said suspiciously.

"You'll need to look after her." Again he paused. "If she lives, she'll be the fastest creature in the world. The female falcon is bigger, stronger, and faster than the male."

"Well, that's as it should be," muttered Pirra.

"A falcon is proud and quick to take offense. She never forgets an insult. You can't tame her and you can't punish her into obedience. You can only gain her trust, and persuade her to stay with you." He glanced at Pirra. "And she will *never* try to please. So I thought you two might get along."

Pirra snorted a laugh.

"For now, she's a captive, like you. But if you look after her, you could teach her to fly. You could set her free."

Pirra repressed a spark of excitement. "You've thought it all out, haven't you?" she said drily.

Userref smiled and shook his head. "Not me, Pirra, this is the will of *Heru*. Why else do you think this falcon came to you?"

---

Pirra named her Echo, because of her ringing *eck-eck-eck*. She was clever, moody, and fierce, and she either liked something or she didn't, and that was that.

Luckily, she liked Pirra. She liked Userref too, but she *hated* Silea, and had a horror of ants. If she spotted one, she went into a frenzy and wouldn't calm down till the entire chamber had been searched and rendered antless.

The days sped past, and Pirra forgot everything but

Echo. She kept her chamber dim to reassure the fledgling, and Userref put a log in a corner for a perch, and tied Echo to it with traces of braided lambskin around her legs.

At first the fledgling was nervous, standing tall and glaring with half-open beak. Pirra talked to her and eventually she relaxed, fluffing out her chin-feathers and perching comfortably on one leg, with the other tucked under her belly.

She had astonishing eyesight. She could spot an ant at thirty paces, and would turn her head right around to follow it. And she seemed fascinated by Pirra's clothes. "She sees more colors than we do," said Userref. "They say that to falcons, the green and purple glints on a raven's wing are as bright as a rainbow."

Echo swiftly learned that Pirra meant food, and begged with plaintive wails, *kyi-kyi-kyi*. Her favorite was pigeon: She would pluck out its feathers with her beak, toss away the guts, then hold down the carcass with one foot and rip it to shreds. Later, she'd squirt her droppings into the corner, then sick up a neat pellet of squashed feathers and bone.

With startling speed, she grew from a scruffy fledgling to a handsome falcon, as tall as Pirra's forearm was long. Her head and wings were a beautiful dusky gray, her throat and breast creamy buff speckled with brown. Her large hooked beak could snap a pigeon's spine or bite a chunk out of Pirra's finger—although she never did. And beneath her great black eyes ran the mark of all falcons: a dark vertical stripe, like the track of a tear.

Pirra hated tying her up, so she gave her the run of the chamber—although on Userref's advice, she left the traces on her legs.

"To teach her to fly," he said, "you must gain her trust. Stay with her, talk to her, give her scraps of squirrel to keep her busy. Get her used to your touch."

By now, Echo knew her own name, and sometimes when Pirra called, she hopped off her perch and came running, her talons clicking on the floor. Once, when Pirra left the chamber, Echo called to her: *eck-eck-eck.*

At first, Pirra stroked her with a feather, then the back of her finger, over her cool soft breast and down her scaly yellow-green feet. Echo seemed to like having her feet stroked best.

One day, as Pirra was stroking her ankles, the falcon stepped calmly onto her fist. Pirra felt a prickling of awe. For all Echo's endearing ways, she was a creature of the Goddess.

"Keep your elbow close to your side and your forearm level," Userref said quietly from the doorway, "that'll make a comfortable perch. Don't let go of the traces."

Echo was heavier than she looked, and her talons dug into Pirra's flesh like slender black thorns.

"I'll make a leather cuff to protect your wrist," said Userref. "And from now on, you should carry a pouch with scraps of meat, for rewards."

"How come you know so much about falcons?" said Pirra without taking her eyes off Echo.

"All Egyptians know about falcons. My brother Nebetku taught me. He knew more than most."

"Did he have a tame one?"

"Remember, you never *tame* a falcon! You just persuade her to stay with you for a while."

Pirra wanted to know what he meant by a while, but Userref had gone back to his chamber. It made him sad to talk of his brother; they'd been close before Userref was taken for a slave.

That night, Echo roosted on the bedpost by Pirra's head, and Pirra lay listening to her doing her evening preen: brisk little rustlings and beak-clickings, then a snap of shaken-out feathers as she settled to sleep. Pirra felt better than she had since she'd been brought to Taka Zimi.

Next day, she took Echo into the courtyard for the first time. Silea and the guards were banished indoors, and Pirra and Userref watched the falcon hop about to explore. She pecked everything, and seemed fascinated by the juniper tree on the lookout post. When the wind gusted, she flapped her wings.

"She ought to be flying by now," said Userref. "Maybe she lost her confidence, falling out of her nest."

"How can I help her?" said Pirra.

"Be patient. It shouldn't be long."

"When she does fly—will she come back?"

"Oh, yes. She can't hunt yet, and she thinks of this place

as her eyrie. She'll fly around, learning to use her wings, but she'll keep coming back."

Pirra shot him a glance. "Always?"

"No," he said gently. "Once she's made her first kill, she'll be gone."

Pirra went cold inside. "When? When will she make her first kill?"

He hesitated. "A few days. Maybe longer."

Pirra put her hand to her mouth. Only *days*? "Well," she faltered. "That's as it should be. I want her to be free."

But that night, as she gazed at the falcon on the bedpost, she said, "Don't leave me, Echo. I can't be here without you."

Echo paused in her preening and glanced at her, and in her dark eyes, Pirra glimpsed the wildness of high places where she could never go.

The next day was blustery, with snow swirling in the courtyard. Echo was restless, flapping her wings at every gust.

All at once, she bobbed her head up and down, shook out her feathers, spread her wings—and *flew*.

Pirra felt a sharp tug in her heart as Echo rose with a joyful shriek, wobbled, then glided over the sanctuary wall.

Echo flew higher—and for a moment, to Pirra's astonishment, she felt as if she was flying with Echo: rushing through the limitless Sky.

She felt as if she was free.

The falcon rode the Wind and shrieked with joy. She was a *falcon*, this was what she was *for*!

In places the Wind flowed fast and smooth, but in others it was bumpy, with sudden drops and peaks. The falcon couldn't see them but she felt them, and she had fun twisting and turning: tilting her wingtips to slide off a bumpy bit, slowing herself down by spreading her tail feathers, then stretching her wings and letting an updraft carry her higher.

The strings on her legs dragged a little, but she forgot them as she soared and the earth fell away. The girl was a speck—and yet the falcon felt her spirit flying with her.

Suddenly, the falcon's heart leaped. There, far below: *pigeons.*

Folding her wings and tucking her feet under her tail, she dived, enjoying the rush of the freezing air.

The pigeons were fast and they'd seen her. They darted confusingly, she couldn't decide which one to attack. The Wind was lumpy and tangled. She struggled to adjust her wing feathers to keep her plunge straight.

Just before she reached them, she thrust out her legs and clenched her feet to knock one out of the Sky . . .

She missed.

Pretending it hadn't happened, she flew off. She was outraged. She was *ashamed*. What had she done wrong?

Through the voices of Wind and snow and the flurry of escaping pigeons, she heard the girl calling, and flew back toward the eyrie.

The girl didn't mind that she'd missed. The falcon swooped down, skimming so low that her wing beats stirred the girl's hair, and the girl laughed, which made the falcon feel a bit better, so she swept off to the juniper tree for a rest.

Perched snugly out of the Wind in the dense branches, she did some preening, then realized she was hungry. The girl always had meat, so the falcon launched off again to get some.

*Something yanked her back.*

Startled, the falcon struggled to free herself. She couldn't. The strings on her legs had become tangled in the branches. The falcon tried to peck herself free, but the juniper was prickly and thick; she couldn't reach.

She shrieked and gaped in alarm. She was stuck.

# 7

"She'll come down when she's hungry," said Userref. "Until then, you'd better leave her in peace."

"Mm," Pirra said doubtfully.

They knew Echo was in the juniper tree, but it was so dense that they couldn't see her, and when Pirra called, all she heard was a shriek, which could mean anything. Reluctantly, she followed Userref inside.

But Echo didn't come down, and Pirra couldn't sleep. She had a horrible tangled-up feeling, as if she was trapped and unable to move. Maybe Echo was trapped. Maybe she *couldn't* come down.

As night wore on, the trapped feeling grew worse, and Pirra became more and more convinced that Echo was in trouble. She had to be rescued.

The wind had dropped, and the courtyard was cold and still. In the torchlight, the bulls' horns cast spiky shadows on the snow.

To avoid getting snagged in the branches, Pirra took off her cloak, boots, and socks and left them at the foot of the wall. The pegs were icy beneath her bare feet as she climbed to the lookout post, and a freezing wind swept up from the precipice.

The sky was just beginning to turn gray, and the juniper was dark and forbidding. Pirra had never climbed a tree in her life. If she made a wrong move, it would be her last.

It occurred to her that Hylas would have sped up it like a squirrel. *Oh, shut up,* she told herself. *He isn't here.*

The first branch she grabbed snapped, nearly pitching her over the edge. Breathing hard, she seized another, and clawed and scrabbled her way into the tree.

"Echo?" she panted.

No answer. But she was here, Pirra felt it.

The juniper was gritty with ash, and as she climbed higher, Pirra got liberally scratched and her feet went numb with cold. At last, through the branches, she glimpsed feathers.

Echo was perched just out of reach, her head hunched on her shoulders, fast asleep. In the gloom, Pirra saw that her traces were badly snagged. No wonder she couldn't get down.

She was about to call to her when Echo stirred in her sleep. Pirra gasped. The falcon's right eye was shut, but her left eye was open and alert. One half of her slept—while the other remained awake.

Once again, it came to Pirra that Echo wasn't just a tetchy young falcon, but a sacred creature whose spirit could never be wholly known.

"She is a daughter of *Heru* the All-Seeing," Userref had

told her. "*Heru* the Great Falcon, Lord of the Horizons. The speckled feathers of His breast are the stars, and His wings are the sky: With every downbeat He creates the winds. *Heru* never sleeps, for His left eye is the Moon, and his right eye is the Sun, which gives life to all . . ."

Somewhere far beyond the Great Cloud, the Sun woke—and so did Echo. She sneezed, tried to scratch her ear with one foot, realized she was stuck, and struggled to flap her wings.

"Keep still, you'll hurt yourself!" said Pirra. "I'll cut you free."

Echo swiveled her head and glared at her. Her beak was agape, sending out smoky puffs of breath, but she was listening.

Still talking, Pirra stretched as far as she could, and offered Echo a scrap of frozen squirrel. Echo relaxed enough to take it, and while she was ripping it to shreds, Pirra drew her knife and cut the traces.

To her surprise, instead of taking off, Echo gulped the rest of the squirrel, then sidled along the branch and stepped onto her wrist. For a moment, Pirra put her forehead against the falcon's cool soft breast, and felt Echo's beak touch her hair. "Thank you, Echo," she whispered.

Then the falcon was gone, swooping down to the courtyard, where she perched on the woodpile and called impatiently to Pirra. *Eck-eck-eck! Hurry up and come down!*

Stiff with cold, Pirra scrambled out of the tree and down to the courtyard. She'd pulled on her clothes and was dusting herself off when Userref and Silea emerged from the sanctuary.

The Egyptian saw Echo and smiled. "I told you she'd come down when she was ready."

Pirra didn't reply.

Silea was eyeing her suspiciously. "Mistress, you have juniper prickles in your hair."

"So I have," Pirra said coolly.

---

A few days later, Echo flew off and didn't come back.

Since being rescued from the tree, her flying had improved incredibly fast, with agile swerves and heart-stopping drops. Pirra had worried that she'd crash, until Userref had pointed out the extra feathers on the elbows of her wings: "They'll slow her down till she can handle an adult's speed."

But suddenly Echo wasn't there anymore. Pirra stood in the courtyard, unable to take it in. She had a sense of a high, cold, limitless sky, and knew that Echo was far away. "I didn't think she'd go so soon," she whispered.

"She may still return," said Userref.

"But it's been a whole day, and she hasn't learned to hunt!"

"The Wild is her home, Pirra. She'll learn. And who knows, maybe she'll bring back the Sun."

Pirra didn't care about the Sun; she wanted Echo.

When Userref had gone inside, she climbed to the lookout post. Clouds seeped over the crags, and the pines stood silent on the slopes. Behind the waterfall's muted roar, she sensed the vast brooding presence of the mountain. She was alone again. Trapped in this endless gray twilight.

Without Echo, her chamber was deathly quiet. The remains of a pigeon wing dangled from the bedpost, and on the floor stood a small earthenware dish of water. Echo had ignored it—Userref said falcons rarely drank—but Pirra had found this so hard to believe that she'd put it there anyway.

Beside it lay one of Echo's pellets, delicately woven of mouse fur and bones. Pirra stooped to put it in her amulet pouch—and suddenly the floor tilted, a wave of weakness washed over her, and her knees buckled and she went down.

The next thing she knew, she was lying in bed. Userref was tucking sheepskins around her, and Silea was warming a bowl over the brazier.

The glow of the embers hurt Pirra's eyes. "Wha' happened?" she mumbled.

"It's nothing," Userref said in a low voice. "You caught a fever, being out in the cold."

It didn't feel like nothing. Her head was cracking open and she was freezing and burning up at the same time.

When she woke again, she ached all over, her teeth were chattering, and needles of fire were piercing her skull.

Userref sat cross-legged on the ground, rocking and muttering a charm in Egyptian. He'd reverted to his old linen kilt, and on his bare chest she saw his *wedjat* amulet:

the sacred eye of his falcon-headed god. Over the winter, he'd taught Pirra a little of his speech, and she understood snatches of the charm. *"My fledgling is hot in the nest . . . the black seeds of sickness fly towards her . . . All-seeing One, let them not touch her . . ."*

Pirra shut her eyes, but that made her dizzier. She spiraled down into the whirling dark . . .

Now Hylas was bending over her, scowling through his shaggy fair hair. "What have you done with Havoc?" he demanded. "You were supposed to look after her!"

"I lost her," she mumbled.

"This always happens," he complained. "I make friends, then I lose them. But this time, it's your fault!"

What about me? she wanted to say. You didn't *lose* me, you sent me away.

But she was so weak her lips wouldn't move, and the pain in her head was agonizing. She tried to tell him that she was sorry about Havoc, but as she squinted up at him, he turned into Silea. The slave girl was clutching a steaming basin and shaking with terror. "I c-can't touch her," she stammered. "I'll catch it too!"

"Give that to me," snapped Userref. Snatching the basin, he dipped in the cloth and gently wiped Pirra's face. She moaned, and he put down the basin and began passing his cool fingers lightly over her throat, then under her chin, as if he was searching for something.

With a jolt of terror, Pirra realized what he was feeling for: the telltale boils of Plague.

# 8

From a distance, Hylas scanned the farmhouse for signs of Plague. No white handprints, no stumpy little pus-eaters. Should he risk looking inside for food, or press on into the foothills?

*She's in the mountains at Taka Zimi,* Gorgo had said. But *where?* Above him the peaks were covered in snow and riven by deep forested gorges. Pirra could be anywhere. If she was still alive. And if the Plague could kill High Priestess Yassassara, what hope was there for her daughter?

But he had to keep trying. He had sent Pirra to Keftiu. It was his fault that she was shut up in Taka Zimi.

For three days he had made his way across the haunted plain. Once it had been rich and populous, but the ash-gray settlements were deserted—except for half-seen ghosts, angrily seeking what was lost.

He couldn't always see them. At times, a bird or a fox would flee in terror from something unseen; but at others, he would get that ache in his temple, like a warning, and fear would clutch at his heart, and he would glimpse a shadow at the corner of his eye. Why him? Was it because he was here on Keftiu? Was it because of the Plague? All he knew was that it happened, and he hated it.

And he dreaded the Plague. For three days he'd kept to the woods, making shelters out of branches and waking often and checking himself for the black swarm of sickness. To ward it off, he dusted his face with Gorgo's fleabane and sulfur, and scoured his fingertips with a lump of pumice Periphas had given him. "Plague gets in through the whorls on your fingertips," Periphas had said. "You'll increase your chances if you rub them off."

Sometimes, Hylas had spotted other ragged wanderers, but when he'd tried to ask about Taka Zimi, they'd fled. Maybe they thought *he* was a ghost. It was hard to tell in this twilight, because ghosts have no shadow, and without the Sun, neither did anyone else.

He kept stumbling upon tombs. Many had been hastily sealed, and foxes had broken in and scavenged the dead. To stop the ghosts from following him, he'd made wristbands with strips cut from his food pouch, and stained them red with ochre he'd dug from a hill.

His food was getting low. In the few farmhouses that weren't stricken, the fleeing peasants had left little behind. He'd survived on Periphas' bag of barley meal, with milk from a lonely and very sooty goat, which had been so glad to be milked that he hadn't had the heart to kill it. It had repaid him by uprooting its tether and sneaking off while he slept.

It was achingly cold. By now it should be spring, with

bees buzzing in the almond blossom; but the trees and vineyards stood silent and black. If the Sun didn't return soon, nothing would grow and everyone would starve. Gorgo was right. The gods had abandoned Keftiu.

The farmhouse door creaked dismally in the wind. *Could* he risk going inside?

He was too hungry to care, and headed for the door.

He was in luck. Whoever had lived here had forgotten two smoke-blackened pig's legs, hanging from a cross-beam.

As he reached to unhook them, a pigeon burst from the rafters with a clatter of wings, and he caught movement in the shadows. Whipping out his knife, he leaped sideways. A pitchfork skewered the wall where he'd stood a moment before.

His attacker jabbed at him again, yelling in Keftian.

Again Hylas dodged. "I don't want to fight!" he shouted.

Still yelling, the Keftian lunged. He was a ragged young man with a grimy, desperate face: clearly a wanderer like Hylas, also after that meat.

"I don't want to *fight*!" repeated Hylas, yanking his axe from his belt.

Shouting and brandishing weapons, they glared at each other.

"This is *stupid*!" panted Hylas. "There's enough for both of us!"

The Keftian scowled and shook his pitchfork. For all he knew, Hylas was threatening to gut him like a pig.

With his knife, Hylas pointed at a pig leg, then at his own chest. "That one for me and that one"—he pointed at the other—"for you."

With a snarl, the Keftian stood his ground.

To prove his good faith, Hylas tossed over his waterskin. "Have a drink. It's milk." He uttered *ug-ug* noises, then pulled imaginary teats, made the *ffft-ffft* sound of milk hitting a pail, and bleated like a goat.

Fear and hunger warred in the Keftian's face. Without taking his eyes off Hylas, he snatched the waterskin and sniffed. He took a gulp.

"*Ug-ug*," urged Hylas as he slowly sheathed his knife.

The Keftian set down the waterskin and stared at him.

Hylas laid his axe on the floor, then raised his hands, palms outward. "See? No weapons."

A long, taut silence. Still with his eyes on Hylas, the Keftian propped his pitchfork against the wall. Then he put his fist to his forehead, bowed—and broke into a grin.

Some time later, after they'd eaten their fill and made rope slings to carry their pig's legs, Hylas and the Keftian went outside and gazed at the mountains.

Keftian mountains were nothing like the ones where Hylas had grown up. Lykonian mountains were jagged, but Keftian peaks were rounded; they made Hylas think of gods lying on their backs and staring at the sky.

"*Dikti*," said the Keftian, pointing at the top of the highest mountain. "*Taka Zimi, Dikti.*"

"That's the mountain's name?" said Hylas. "Dikti?"

The Keftian nodded. "*Taka Zimi. Dikti.*"

Hylas put his fist to his forehead and bowed. "Thank you."

The Keftian indicated that he intended to stay in the farmhouse, and after more bowing, Hylas headed off.

He hadn't gone far when the Keftian called to him again. "*Rauko!*" he shouted. Then he stamped one foot, raised both outstretched arms to his ears, and pointed forward. "*Rauko, rauko!*"

Puzzled, Hylas shook his head. *What do you mean?*

The Keftian did it again. When Hylas still didn't understand, the Keftian gave up and bowed. That looked suspiciously like *Good luck, you're going to need it*—and as Hylas headed for the mountains, he sensed that he'd been given a warning.

*They say there's Plague up that way,* Gorgo had told him, *and some monster stalking the forest.*

Was that what the Keftian had been trying to tell him? *Beware of monsters?*

⸻

Hylas encountered no monsters, but as he climbed higher, every hut and farmhouse bore the marks of Plague.

He wondered if Pirra had been with her mother when she'd died. Pirra had hated her mother, but how would she feel now? Hylas had never known his own mother, who'd left him and Issi on Mount Lykas when they were little, and he'd envied Pirra hers. She'd always found that hard to understand.

He found a trail that followed a stream up a gully, and came to a grove of ash-crusted olive trees. Near one, he found a muddy wallow, and at about the height of his head, a patch of bark rubbed off the trunk. What creature had done this? A bear would have left claw marks, but there were none. A deer? Hylas didn't know any that big.

A monster?

At the head of the gully, he made out a derelict farm: a dung heap, a stone cistern, a mud-brick hut. From thirty paces, the white handprint on the door of the hut shouted "Plague."

But the stream looked clear, and its banks were thick with willows; Hylas even spotted a few patches of green grass. It was such a relief to see green after the endless gray that he took this as a good omen, and kneeled to refill his waterskin.

He stiffened. Beside his knee was a hoof print bigger than his head.

Quietly, he rose to his feet. Near a clump of boulders a few paces off, he saw a vast mound of steaming droppings.

At that moment, he heard a snort, and from behind the boulders stepped an enormous cow and her giant calf.

His belly turned over. The cow had the vicious forward-pointing horns of wild cattle. He'd encountered them in the mountains where he'd grown up. They were twice as big as tame cattle, and twice as mean. And this one had seen him.

"It's all right," he told the cow quietly. "I'm not going to bother you or your calf."

The cow lifted her huge blunt muzzle and tasted his scent.

"I'm going to move slowly away from you," said Hylas, doing just that. "I—I can't climb out of the gully on this side, it's too steep, so I'm going to cross the stream and climb out over there, see? Where it's not so steep? I'm not coming anywhere near you."

The cow decided he was no threat, and put down her head to drink.

Hylas was halfway across the stream when he heard a rustling directly ahead, and from the willows stepped the biggest bull he'd ever seen.

Its horns were over an arm span wide and its hide was matted with foul-smelling ash; it had been rolling in its own urine. Bulls do that when their blood is up, and they're spoiling for a fight.

In horror, Hylas took in its flaring nostrils and hot red-rimmed eyes. *This* was what the Keftian had been trying to tell him, pawing the earth with his foot and pointing his arms: *Like horns. Rauko, rauko.* Bull.

All this flashed through his mind in a heartbeat. He couldn't climb out of the gully, the bull was blocking his way, and—which was much, much worse—*he* was in *its* way.

Without meaning to, he'd put himself between the bull and its mate.

# 9

The bull didn't paw the earth as the Keftian had done. It just charged.

Dropping his waterskin, Hylas raced for the hut with the bull thundering after him. He made for the cistern, hoping to leap from there to the roof. It was too far, he'd never do it. He grabbed a pitchfork lying on the ground, took a run at the hut, jammed the butt of the pitchfork in the earth, and tried to vault onto the roof.

He didn't quite make it and clung to the edge, scrabbling with his feet. Moments before the bull struck, he hauled himself up. One horn missed his boot by a hand's breadth and gouged a furrow in the wall.

Thatch came out in handfuls as Hylas crawled farther up the roof. He saw the bull swing around for another attempt. Surely it wouldn't attack a *house*?

The great beast's head slammed into the wall, scattering chunks of mud-brick and sending a shudder through the roof.

Shaken and out of breath, Hylas watched it trot off for another attack. He still had his axe, knife, slingshot, and the pig's leg slung across his back. None of these would be much good against an angry bull.

The hut on which he perched was close to the steep side of the gully, which was sheer rock, impossible to climb. He *had* to reach the other side across the stream—but to do that, he had to get past the bull.

Another crash shook the hut, and the bull bellowed, furious that it couldn't reach its foe.

Hylas crawled higher. If he could distract the beast, he *might* have time to make it across the stream.

Below him, on the side of the hut the bull couldn't see, he spotted an abandoned cart. Its two shafts pointed downward, like the horns of a grazing beast. That gave him an idea.

While the bull cantered away for another charge, Hylas slid off the roof and swiftly tied one of his red wristbands to the cart-shaft, then propped both shafts on a log, so that they pointed forward, like a bull leveling its head to attack.

The earth shook with the thunder of hooves, and Hylas jumped from cart to roof. Yanking out a handful of thatch, he leaned down and waved it at the bull. "Hey you!" he yelled.

The bull jolted to a halt and glared up at him.

"There's another bull round the back!" shouted Hylas, trailing the thatch. "He's after your female!"

The bull swung its massive head from side to side. Then it charged Hylas' handful of thatch—and chased it around the corner of the hut.

The bull saw the cart and again jolted to a halt. It saw the red wristband flapping in the wind. It snorted, pawed the earth—and charged.

Praying it would be too busy to notice him, Hylas slid off the other side and splashed across the stream, snatching his waterskin as he went, then scrambled up the side of the gully to safety.

He glanced back once, and saw the cow and her calf solemnly watching their master savage the cart to splinters.

———

Two days later, Hylas found a cave and made camp for the night.

At a frozen stream he broke the ice with his axe and filled his waterskin; then he woke a fire inside the cave and huddled over it, chewing a chunk of pig's leg.

He was exhausted, and he missed Periphas. In some ways, the Messenian reminded him of Akastos, the mysterious wanderer he'd encountered in the past. Both had fled homelands invaded by the Crows; both could be harsh and withdrawn, but they had been roughly kind to Hylas.

He was cold too. The mountains were deep in snow. His legs ached from laboring up snowbound gorges and through steep forests of silent pines.

And he was frightened. He'd come upon few huts and fewer ghosts, and yet a sense of dread had been growing on him all day. He dreaded the monster Gorgo had warned him about. It couldn't have been the bull, she must know about wild bulls, and she wouldn't have called it a monster. So what was it?

He feared the Crows too. Gorgo had mistaken him for a Crow spy—so she must regard them as a threat. The Crows' stronghold was far away across the Sea, but they were a mighty clan, and now that they had their dagger back, they would be even stronger.

Was it possible that they were here, on Keftiu?

The fire cast leaping shadows on the cave wall. Sleepily, Hylas made a shadow-rabbit with his hand. He used to do that for Issi, especially in winter, when the nights were long. They used to play at warriors with icicles as swords, and Issi had been a lethal shot with a snowball.

But most of all, she loved water. The summer she'd turned six, he'd taught her to swim with a blown-up goat bladder for a float. In half a day, she'd been better than him, and after that she was always in any stream or lake they came upon. He used to tease her that she'd grow webbed feet, like her beloved frogs . . .

He woke with a start to the chill certainty that he wasn't alone.

He heard harsh, panting breath. In the dark at the back of the cave, something moved.

Drawing his knife and seizing a burning brand, Hylas swept the shadows. He caught the gleam of eyes. His blood ran cold. Wolf? Bear? *Monster?*

Suddenly the creature sped past him. Hylas flung himself against the wall. As the creature fled the cave, it glanced back, and he glimpsed matted fur, huge golden eyes—and a scar across its nose.

His heart lurched. "*Havoc?*" he cried.

# 10

The boy stood at the mouth of his lair, peering into the Dark. He couldn't see her, the lion cub was certain.

*Was* it the boy who'd looked after her long ago?

When she'd caught his scent lower down the mountain, it had scratched at her heart and she'd been desperate to go to him. Fear had taken over—but she hadn't been able to make herself leave, so she'd followed him through the not-Light and into the Dark. She'd even padded into his lair and sniffed him while he slept. She still didn't know if it was him.

His scent had changed. It was more like that of a full-grown man, and he also smelled strongly of sheep, which was odd. He never used to smell of sheep.

He looked different too. He was broader, and as tall as a tree. Worst of all, he didn't *sound* like the boy she had known; his voice was much deeper.

As the lion cub went off to hunt, her wariness grew. This boy was scared of her, but the boy who'd looked after her long ago had never been scared.

And the boy in the lair had lashed out at her with fire

and his big shiny claw. So even if he *was* the same boy, he had become like all the others.

He was just another human. And the lion cub would never trust a human, not ever again.

---

Was it really Havoc? wondered Hylas as he followed the paw prints through the snow.

He'd glimpsed a young lion. But had he really seen that scar on her nose? Even if he had, lots of lions had scars.

He tried to remember if Pirra had ever said there were lions on Keftiu. He thought she'd said there weren't, but if he was wrong . . .

One thing was certain: Those paw prints in the cave were real. While he slept, she'd stood right over him. Surely no other lion would have done that?

It began to snow. To the west, the slope fell away to a forested saddle that looked as if it led to the peak of Mount Dikti. Pirra was somewhere up there; but the trail of paw prints climbed *south*, toward a rocky ridge that led away from the peak.

Pirra needed him—but so did Havoc. The lion cub was only a yearling; she couldn't survive for long with no pride to help her hunt. And it was his fault that she was here on Keftiu.

Hylas rubbed his chin and stomped in circles. If this snow kept up, those tracks wouldn't last long. He blew out a long breath. "I'm sorry, Pirra," he said out loud. "I will come and find you. But I have to find Havoc first."

He hadn't climbed far up the ridge when he came upon a grimy little pus-eater glaring down at him from a boulder.

His breath smoked in the frosty air, and around him the pines stood watchful and silent.

By now he'd learned that Keftians put pus-eaters not only by dwellings, but also by tombs, to catch the Plague wafting from the newly dead. Sure enough, a little farther on, he spotted a small tomb cut into the ridge. Whoever had sealed it had been in a hurry. Stones had been clawed away from the entrance, and to judge from the harsh croaks of ravens, the corpse inside had been dragged out by hungry scavengers.

A dreadful thought occurred to Hylas. Had Havoc become a man-eater?

His boots crunched in the stillness as he detoured around the pus-eater and followed the paw prints toward the tomb. Ravens flew away with loud caws, and a fox slunk off.

Havoc didn't. She lay tensely on her belly with her head between her shoulder blades. Watching him.

It was her. She'd doubled in size since last year, and her fur was thick and shaggy, but he saw how thin she was underneath. She was still a cub—a gawky yearling—who must have survived by scavenging what she could. Was that why she'd hunkered down near the bones of the human dead?

*No*, thought Hylas. *I won't believe it. She can't be a man-eater, not Havoc.*

"Havoc?" he called softly. "It's me, Hylas. Do you remember me?"

Havoc lashed her tail and hissed, baring huge white fangs. Her eyes were colder than he'd ever seen them, and she stared at him without recognition.

"Havoc, what's happened to you?"

Her huge claws kneaded the snow, as if she was getting ready to spring.

His hand went to his knife. This can't be, he thought.

With a snarl she sprang away and vanished like a ghost among the pines.

"Havoc!" he shouted.

She didn't come back. She hadn't recognized him.

---

The lion cub fled up the mountain with the boy's yowls fading behind her. It was him, she was sure of it. She remembered his eyes and his lion-colored mane—and she sensed the lion in his spirit. But he'd changed, she was sure of that too. He was almost a man. And she would never trust a human, not ever again.

As she slowed to a trot, things clawed at her heart that made her snarl. She remembered lying with her head on his legs while he scratched behind her ears. And climbing trees and getting stuck, and him helping her down.

The Bright Soft Cold was hissing harder now, and the wind was beginning to growl. How would the boy survive? There were bears and wolves on the mountain, and like all humans, he was puny. If anything hurt him . . .

The lion cub spun around and raced back down the slope.

When she caught the boy's scent, she slowed to a walk. She couldn't go near him, but she could follow him and make sure that he came to no harm. And at least it would be easy to stay hidden; like all humans, he didn't notice much and couldn't smell.

The not-Light gave way to the Dark again, and the Bright Soft Cold pelted the mountain. The wind howled in fury—and still the cub followed, slitting her eyes against the storm.

The boy was in trouble. He was staggering, and his fur-less face was turning gray. The lion cub knew that despite his sheep-like overpelt, he couldn't just curl up under a boulder as she could, and sleep till the wind calmed down.

If she didn't lead him to safety, he would die.

———

You should've known better, Hylas told himself as he struggled through the blizzard.

He'd grown up in mountains and survived countless blizzards. Why hadn't he had more sense? At the first sign of a storm, he should've found shelter, woken a fire, and waited it out; but in his eagerness to find Havoc, he'd plodded on, and now night was falling and he was so cold that his thoughts were beginning to blur. If he didn't get under cover fast, he would die.

A flash of movement between the trees—and there was Havoc, not ten paces away, watching him.

"*Havoc*," he mumbled, but his voice was lost in the screaming wind.

Havoc turned and headed off at a muscular trot with her tail held high. She glanced back. Did she want him to follow?

Knee-deep, he floundered after her. Again she waited, then trotted off, her tail-tuft showing black against the snow.

And so it went for an endless time. Snow stung Hylas' face, and every step became a struggle. At last he halted, panting and swaying. He caught a whiff of woodsmoke. *Woodsmoke?* Out here?

Havoc returned and lifted her head, as if to say *Hurry up*.

Nearly spent, Hylas labored on for a few more steps. Between the trees, he glimpsed a blocky shadow. *A hut.*

A few more steps and he made out a small hide window: a glowing red kernel of warmth in the freezing darkness of the storm. He staggered toward it. Couldn't take another step. He shouted, but the roar of the storm drowned his voice. He sank to his knees. He couldn't reach the door, he was spent.

He lay on his back, watching the snow hurtling toward him out of the black night sky. But now through the whirling whiteness, two great amber eyes were gazing down at him. "Havoc," he croaked.

Warm meaty breath heated his face. A big black nose brushed his cheek, and he felt the prickle of whiskers.

Clumsily, he put up his hand and clutched shaggy fur.

"*Havoc . . .*"

The door creaked open and firelight washed over him.

Havoc slipped from his grip and fled into the night just before Hylas blacked out.

# 11

Hylas is dreaming that someone's brushing snow off his face.

"You should be ashamed of yourself, Flea," growls the man in the dream. "Mountain boy like you, getting caught in a snowstorm!"

That voice: strong, smooth, startlingly familiar. Hylas' heart leaps. "*Akastos?*"

"Shut up and drink this." A spout is jammed between Hylas' teeth, and he chokes on vinegary wine. He can't see, but he's sure it's Akastos: wanderer, blacksmith, exile, murderer haunted by the spirits of vengeance. Hylas admires him more than any man he's ever met. He doesn't want this dream to end.

"Stop grinning, Flea, you're dribbling."

Hylas gives a spluttery laugh. It's so good to hear the nickname Akastos gave him once. If only this dream would last . . .

He woke up. Akastos was still there. "It's really you!" cried Hylas.

"Well of course it is," snapped Akastos.

He was sitting on a log by a roaring fire. Steam rose from his sheepskins and his grimy fur cloak, and snow speckled his beard and his long, dark tangled hair. His light-gray eyes were as keen as ever, and fixed suspiciously on Hylas. "Why were you following me?" he demanded.

Hylas struggled to sit up. "I wasn't. I didn't even know you were on Keftiu, I was following Havoc—"

"*Havoc?*" Akastos was startled. "That lion cub is on Keftiu?"

"She led me here, she must have known it was you. She saved me . . ." He trailed off. It was warm in the hut, but outside, the blizzard was raging, the wind roaring in the pines, making the roof beams creak. Havoc was out there alone.

"A lion led you to me," murmured Akastos, scratching his beard in a gesture Hylas remembered. "I wonder what that means."

"I don't know, but I'm glad she did. And I'm *really* glad you got away from Thalakrea!"

Akastos sighed. "I suppose I'm glad you did too, Flea."

"Why only suppose?"

The wanderer stared at him. "How can you ask? *Fifteen years* I've been on the run from the Crows. I had *one chance* to kill a highborn Crow. *One chance* to destroy the dagger of Koronos. What happens? You. And you think I'd be glad to see you?"

"Then why rescue me?" Hylas said sulkily.

"Because for some reason I couldn't let you freeze to death outside the door." He rose to fetch wood from a pile in the corner, and Hylas saw how he winced and flexed his right leg. "Yes that's your fault too," muttered Akastos. "A little reminder of that burn you gave me last summer."

"Sorry."

"That's not going to do me much good. Here, help fix something to eat."

Hylas rummaged around and found two chipped horn beakers and a couple of bowls, while Akastos unearthed a soot-crusted cooking pot and pooled their provisions: what was left of the barley meal and bacon, some goat's cheese, a couple of moldy onions, snow, and a handful of hairy pale-green leaves from a pouch at his belt.

"What's that?" Hylas said warily.

"Dittany. It only grows in the Keftian mountains and it keeps away Plague—so don't complain about the taste." Chucking Hylas a stick, he told him to stir the porridge, then started mixing wine with more snow and crumbled cheese in another bowl.

Hylas said, "There's something I need to tell you."

"Mm."

"They—the Crows—they got the dagger back."

Akastos stopped mixing the wine. "How?" he said.

Hylas told him how he'd battled the Crows on the burning mountain of Thalakrea. He was shaking when he'd finished, but Akastos merely lifted his beaker and tasted the wine, then wiped his mouth on the back of his hand.

"You don't seem surprised," said Hylas.

"I'm not. I guessed months ago, because they're stronger than ever. They've taken the mines at Lavrion—which means they can make all the weapons they need." He paused. "Now suppose you tell me how you fetched up here."

Still stirring the porridge, Hylas told him of his wanderings, and Akastos listened without giving anything away, although he asked lots of questions about Periphas.

"When we reached Keftiu," said Hylas, "the others left and I stayed . . ." He broke off, remembering the haunted shore and the ghostly children. "Something's wrong with me," he blurted out. "I can see ghosts."

Akastos set down his beaker and looked at him.

"It's horrible, I hate it!" cried Hylas. "I never know when I'm going to see them—and when I do, my head hurts." He touched the scar on his temple. "Why is it happening? Why me? I never could before!" He appealed to Akastos, the wisest man he knew.

But all the wanderer said was, "You still haven't told me what you're doing here."

Hylas blinked. "I—I'm trying to find Pirra."

"Who? Oh, I remember, your girl."

Hylas flushed. "She's not my girl, we're just friends."

Akastos snorted. "You're what, nearly fourteen? You expect me to believe that?"

Hylas' flush deepened. "I don't care what you believe," he said crossly. "She's somewhere called Taka Zimi, it's high on Mount Dikti, but I don't know where."

"Stop stirring, it's ready," said Akastos.

The wine was strong, the porridge delicious, and Hylas forgot about being annoyed and ate two bowlfuls, then scraped the pot. Feeling pleasantly giddy and beautifully warm, he mustered his courage. "What about you?"

"What about me?" said Akastos without looking up.

"What are you doing here?"

He could see Akastos deciding how much to tell him. "I'm trying to find some people I used to know who hate the Crows as much as I do."

The Crows. In his mind, Hylas saw their black rawhide armor and their harsh faces smeared with ash. Out loud he said, "Are the Crows here on Keftiu?"

"If not yet, then soon."

"Why would they come here?"

"Work it out, Flea. After what's happened, Keftiu is the weakest it's been in years. The Crows are bound to invade, it's what they do." His tone was bitter. Long ago, the Crows had invaded his homeland. He'd fought alongside the rightful High Chieftain, and they might have won, if Outsiders from the mountains had fought with them. But the Outsiders had refused, and because of that, the High Chieftain had been killed, Koronos had seized Mycenae, and Akastos had lost his farm and fled.

A gust of wind burst open the door, letting in a blast of snow. Akastos slammed the door shut and Hylas wedged it with a piece of wood. When he sat down again, he was shaking. That felt like a message from the Crows: *Wherever you are, we will find you.*

All winter, he'd tried not to think about them, but now in his mind he saw Koronos, their lizard-eyed leader. He saw Telamon, who'd been his own best friend until he'd turned his back on friendship and sided with his terrible grandfather, Koronos. He saw Koronos' murderous spawn: Pharax, Alekto, and Kreon. And he remembered the terrible night when the Crows had attacked his camp, killing his dog and separating him from Issi.

Thinking of it made him dizzy and sick, and he clutched his upper arm, where the Crows' black obsidian arrowhead had dug into his flesh.

"So now, Flea," said Akastos, wrenching him back from the past. "Once again you just *happen* to cross my path. All I know about you is that you may or may not be the Outsider in the Oracle. It's time to tell me who you really are."

"Wh-what do you mean?" stammered Hylas. "You know who I am, I'm—"

"Where do you come from? Why do our paths keep crossing? Who were your parents?"

"I don't know," said Hylas. "That's the truth. I never knew my father, I don't know anything about him."

Akastos gave him a long, searching stare. "What about your mother?"

"All I remember is she had dark hair and she told me to look after Issi. She left us on Mount Lykas when we were little, wrapped in a bearskin."

Akastos' face didn't move, but Hylas sensed the swift

current of his thoughts. "A bearskin," repeated the wanderer.

Hylas nodded. "I'm certain she meant to come back for us, but something stopped her. I think she's still alive—I mean, I feel it. Someday, she'll find us."

"But she hasn't."

"No."

Again, Akastos scratched his beard.

As Hylas studied his weather-beaten features, a startling idea came to him. It was so astonishing—so wonderful—that his head swam. "You've been to Lykonia, haven't you?" he began carefully. "I mean, where I grew up?"

Akastos flicked him a glance. "What makes you say that?"

"One of the first things you ever said to me was that I was a long way from Mount Lykas."

Akastos' lip curled. "You remember that?"

"I remember everything you've said to me." Hylas took a deep breath. "Are you my father?"

Outside, the wind dropped, as if it was listening. The fire hissed, sending smoke and sparks sweeping through the smoke-hole and into the dark.

Raising his head, Akastos met Hylas' eyes. "No," he said quietly. "I'm not your father."

Hylas clenched his fists. He was desperate for it to be true. "But—you might be," he said, "only you don't know it. You said you had a son my age."

"I said he would have been your age if he'd lived."

"Well—maybe you met my mother on your travels, and—"

"Hylas, I'm dark and you're fair—"

"That doesn't mean anything! When she was carrying me she could've stared at the Sun; they say that gives a baby fair hair! And you once told me that we're alike, you and me, both survivors, both good liars—"

"Hylas, I remember the women I've been with, and I'm certain. I am not your father."

Hylas stared at his empty cup. There was a sick feeling in the pit of his belly. "I wish you were," he mumbled.

"Why would you wish that?" said Akastos with unaccustomed gentleness.

Hylas wanted to say, because he admired Akastos and longed for him to take the place of the shadowy void that was all he felt when he thought of his father. Instead he muttered, "I don't know, I just do."

He became aware that Akastos was moving about, gathering his gear. "What are you doing?" Hylas said uneasily.

"Storm's blown over. It'll be light soon, I'm heading off."

"Can I come with you? Just for a bit."

Akastos looked down at him, and for a moment his hard features softened. "Hylas. I know our fates are entangled in some way neither of us understands, but I also know that when you're with me, things go wrong. It's better we go our separate ways."

"No!" cried Hylas. He lurched to his feet—and swayed.

His head whirling sickeningly, he couldn't keep his balance.

"Lie down," said Akastos. "You'll feel better soon."

"You *drugged* me," muttered Hylas.

"Just a little poppy juice in your wine, to stop you following me. Here." He tucked a small pouch in Hylas' belt. "Some buckthorn, to keep away ghosts."

"You *drugged* me." Hylas subsided onto the floor. His eyelids were so heavy, they wouldn't stay open.

"About Taka Zimi," said Akastos, his voice coming and going in waves. "Follow this ridge we're on west, till you reach a lightning-struck pine. Behind it you'll see a crag split in two, and a waterfall. Make for that. Taka Zimi is just below it on the shoulder of the mountain. Stay as high as you can for as long as you can, and avoid the gorge. And Hylas—watch yourself. Taka Zimi is a sanctuary of the Goddess. It's not a place you simply walk into."

"Don't leave me," Hylas tried to say, but he couldn't move his lips.

When he woke, the fire had burned low. He stumbled out into the cold gray half-light. Windblown snow hissed sadly about his boots. He could see no footprints. All trace of Akastos was gone.

# 12

The lion cub slitted her eyes against the wind and watched the boy stumble back into his lair.

Sadly, she turned and headed up the ridge. He would be all right now. She had saved him by leading him to the black-maned human, who had looked after him, as he'd done in the past. But now she had to leave. It was too dangerous and confusing to stay.

The storm was over, and the forest creatures were coming out of hiding. Redwings chattered in the branches, scattering the cub with Bright Soft Cold. Swiveling her ears, she caught the caws of ravens, and quickened her pace. Ravens only cawed like that when they'd found a carcass.

They scattered when they saw her, but the cub took one sniff at the carcass and drew back, twitching her tail in disgust. It was human, and crawling with the foul black specks that she knew to avoid.

The Dark swallowed the forest, and the lion cub prowled the mountain in search of food. She found no live prey and no more carcasses, not even bones.

At last she caught the crackle of fire and the voices

of men. She was about to flee, when she smelled meat.

Bristling with fear, she padded closer and snuffed the wind. Yes. The muzzle-watering scent of deer blood.

Terror and hunger fought within her. Hunger won. Placing each paw with care, she belly-crawled between the pines.

Another gust of wind carried the humans' scent to her nose. She froze. There between the trees were the terrible men with the flapping black hides who had slaughtered her pride.

Suddenly she was a little cub again, listening to her father's furious roars as the terrible men closed in for the kill. She saw her mother's great golden lifeless eyes . . .

The rich smell of blood tugged her back. These men had meat. And sometimes, humans left scraps.

---

"I saw something," said Telamon. "Over there among the trees."

"Only a deer," growled Kreon.

"No," said Telamon. "It was bigger than that."

"They say there's a monster on Mount Dikti," muttered Ilarkos, Kreon's second-in-command. "The prisoner told me it was sent by the ghost of the High Priestess to protect her daughter."

Telamon gave him a cold stare. "Nothing can protect her from us. Let's go back to camp; the men have put up the tents and I want to question the prisoner again."

To his irritation, Ilarkos didn't obey at once, but sought

confirmation from Kreon, who drew his wolf-fur cloak about him and gave a curt nod.

How dare he, thought Telamon as they crunched through the snow to where the men were burning worm-wood to ward off the Plague. It was *my* idea to come to Keftiu, I made it happen. And *I'm* going to find the dag-ger. Not Kreon.

It made him seethe that the men still viewed him as a boy, who'd not yet killed enough boar to make his own boars'-tusk helmet, and who—to his shame—hadn't yet grown a beard.

All I need, Telamon told himself, is one chance to prove that I'm a man. Then they'll know *I'm* the one they should obey.

The prisoner stood outside their tent, shivering. Telamon swept past him and ducked inside. Kreon was already seated on a log, warming his hands at the brazier. As Telamon drew up another log, the slave brought a large bronze bowl of roast venison, dried anchovies, and figs, and they fell on it, washing it down with steaming beakers of hon-eyed wine.

At last Kreon wiped his fingers on his furs and nodded to Ilarkos, who brought in the prisoner.

The wretch fell to his knees and touched his forehead to the earth. He was bruised, bloodied, and shaking with fear. Telamon had picked him for a guide because he was a goatherd—and so was Hylas. When Telamon saw the terror in the Keftian's brown eyes, he pictured

Hylas kneeling before him, begging for his life.

"How much farther to Taka Zimi?" he asked in the quiet voice that he'd learned from his grandfather Koronos was so much more terrifying than Kreon's bluster.

Ilarkos, who spoke a little Keftian, translated, and the prisoner stammered an answer in his odd bird-like speech. "He says it's no more than a day, my lord."

"He's sure about that," said Telamon.

Ilarkos grunted. "He'd better be."

Pointedly, Telamon stared at Kreon's weapons, piled on his massive ox-hide shield. The prisoner gulped at the hefty spear and sword and the rawhide whip with the bronze spikes, which earlier had taken the skin off his back.

"And the girl will be there, at Taka Zimi?" said Telamon.

". . . He's sure of that too, my lord," said Ilarkos, translating the desperate torrent of speech. "He says the High Priestess sent the girl there when the Plague struck."

"And he knows what'll happen if he's lying," growled Kreon.

"He knows, my lord."

Telamon rose and put his hands on his hips. The Keftian didn't dare look him in the face, but fastened his gaze on Telamon's belt. His eyes widened as he saw the splendid gold plaques on either side of the clasp.

"Yes, they're Keftian," Telamon told him softly. "Once they were part of a wristband that belonged to your High Priestess' daughter. Now they belong to me. What does that tell you about the fate of your precious island?"

Ilarkos started to translate, but Telamon cut him short. "He understands."

"Take him away and feed him," said Kreon. "We need him alive till we've got the girl."

When the prisoner had been hauled outside, Telamon remained on his feet, warming his hands over the brazier.

Kreon rose, a bull of a man, towering over him. "This is starting to look like a mistake," he said between his teeth.

"Be patient, Uncle," said Telamon.

"I'm not known for my patience. You told me we'd find the dagger. That's why I agreed to come."

Telamon did not reply. It hadn't been hard to persuade Kreon, who was burning to be the one to restore the dagger to his father, Koronos. If he did, then at one stroke he would have gained his father's favor and shattered the hopes of his brother and sister, whom he'd hated all his life.

"And in case you've forgotten," Kreon went on, "if it hadn't been for me, Koronos wouldn't have let you come at all."

"Are you sorry you did?" Telamon said sharply.

"I'm sorry I let you talk us into heading into the mountains! What are we doing here? The House of the Goddess is standing empty, we have a golden chance to seize the whole island!"

"With forty men?"

"Keftians don't know how to fight!" sneered Kreon.

"But instead, where are we? Knee-deep in snow halfway up some cursed mountain—because you say the girl has the dagger!"

"She does."

"You'd better be sure about that."

"I've told you before. I saw her getting away from Thalakrea. I guessed soon afterward that she'd stolen it. Then at Mycenae I asked a seer, and he said, '*What you seek is on Keftiu.*' How much more proof do you need?"

Kreon pushed his face close to Telamon's. "What I *need*," he said in a voice that made Telamon shrink inside, "is to hold the dagger in my fist. What I *need* is to know you're not wasting my time."

Telamon saw the bronze wire glinting in his uncle's greasy black beard. He caught his rank warrior smell and the threat behind his words. If he let Kreon down, kinship wouldn't save him.

What was even more frightening was that beneath his threats, Kreon was scared. Keftiu had turned out to be far more unsettling than either of them had anticipated.

The first night when they'd beached their ships on the coast, they'd smeared their faces with ash and sacrificed a black ram to the Angry Ones. They'd waited for a sign, but it hadn't come. The spirits of air and darkness were far away.

But how was that *possible*? The Angry Ones are drawn to burned things: *Why* would they stay away from a whole vast island reeking of ash?

Telamon had learned the answer from the Keftian prisoner. "When the Great Cloud came and the sky rained ash," the goatherd had babbled, "the High Priestess cast powerful spells to ward off the Angry Ones. Our Keftian magic is ancient, very strong." That hint of defiance had earned him a savage whipping—but his words had struck deep.

"Keftian magic," spat Kreon, as if he'd guessed Telamon's thoughts. With a thick forefinger he jabbed his nephew's chest. "You'd better be sure about this."

"I am," said Telamon with more conviction than he felt.

Soon afterward, Kreon wrapped his cloak about him and threw himself down to sleep. They didn't speak again.

Telamon was restless, so he did the rounds of the camp. Privately, he thought of it as his camp. He was proud of its red wool tents and black-clad warriors—who, after feasting on venison, had turned in, leaving three men on guard.

Once I get the dagger, he thought, you'll take orders from *me*.

He could almost feel the dagger in his hand: the heft of it, the strength it gave its bearer. The first chieftain of the House of Koronos had forged it from the helmet of his slaughtered enemy, and had quenched its burning bronze with blood from his own battle-wounds. So long as the clan possessed it, the House of Koronos could not fall.

"I will get it back," muttered Telamon. "Not Kreon, but *me*."

A gust of wind stirred the branches, sending snow hissing onto his shoulders, and he realized that he'd wandered off among the pines. Despite his wolf-fur mantle and fleece-lined boots, cold seeped into his bones—and doubt.

What if I'm wrong? he thought. What if I'm leading us on a fool's errand to a sanctuary guarded by ancient magic?

Earlier, he'd seen a falcon high in the sky. It had reminded him of Pirra. She had a falcon engraved on her sealstone—and a falcon's sharp dark eyes.

And last night she'd dreamed to him. She'd been with Hylas, who was holding the dagger, and she'd put her hand on Hylas' shoulder, and they'd taunted him: *You can't have it!*

Telamon had woken with tears on his cheeks, feeling horribly left out. The next moment, he'd been furious and ashamed. How dare they invade his dreams?

He still had the scar on his thigh where Pirra had stabbed him last summer. When he caught her, he would even things up and give *her* a scar, then they would both bear each other's mark.

He hated Pirra, but he couldn't stop thinking about her. What she'd said to him on Thalakrea was burned into his brain. *Hylas is strong, but you're weak. I think you'll always be weak.*

He clenched his fists. "You think so, do you?" he muttered. "Well, I'm coming after you, Pirra. And when I find you . . ."

Footsteps crunched in the snow, and Ilarkos loomed behind him, carrying a burning brand. "Thought you might need me, my lord. Not safe on your own with monsters about."

Telamon stiffened. Ilarkos wouldn't have said that to a full-grown warrior. "Do you really believe there's a monster?" he sneered.

Ilarkos shrugged and touched the bow slung over his shoulder. "Doesn't matter what I believe, long as I got this." Suddenly he tensed. "What's that?" he hissed.

Telamon followed his gaze—and caught his breath.

Twenty paces away, in the dark beneath a bush, crouched a patch of lighter shadow.

Fear gripped Telamon's heart. But he had to look strong in front of Ilarkos. "It's not a monster," he breathed. "It— it's a *lion*. Quick, give me your bow!"

"A *lion*?" whispered Ilarkos. "There are no lions on Keftiu!"

"The bow, man, the bow!" The wood was icy to his touch, and his fingers shook as he grabbed an arrow.

The beast in the darkness sensed danger and sprang away—but in the blink of an eye, Telamon had nocked the arrow and let fly. The arrow sang. He heard it strike.

"You hit it!" cried Ilarkos.

Men came running with torches, but when they went to investigate, all they found was a spatter of blood in the snow.

"I did hit it," said Telamon in triumph, "there's the proof!" Snatching a torch, he peered at the trail of paw prints leading up the mountain.

"Good shot, my lord," said Ilarkos. "Will we track it and finish it off?"

Telamon hesitated. "No. The men are tired, and the beast will die without our help, we can go after it in the morning."

Ilarkos bowed. "As you wish, my lord."

Trying to appear calm, Telamon handed him back his bow, but inside, his heart was bursting with pride. *See that, Pirra?* he told her in his head. *I shot a lion. Not so weak now, am I?*

## 13

Pirra was too weak to open her eyes, but she knew at once that she was better. She wasn't burning up and her head didn't hurt.

Snuggling into her sheepskins, she lay luxuriating in the absence of pain. I'm not dead, she thought hazily. I'm not dead . . .

Later, she woke again. Her mouth was so dry, she could hardly swallow, and she was hollow with hunger. "User-ref?" she called. "Silea!"

No answer. Her chamber was dark and cold: The fire in the brazier had been allowed to die. Oh, *Silea!*

Pirra called again, but the slave girl still didn't come—and the water jug was empty. Silea was always "forgetting" to refill it because the cistern was down in the cellar, and she was scared of spirits.

"Oh, *really!*" muttered Pirra, swinging her legs to the floor. Spots swam before her eyes and her blood soughed in her ears. As she waited for it to subside, she saw User-ref's *wedjat* amulet hanging from the bedpost. He must have left it to reassure her, in case she woke before he got back. Putting it around her neck, Pirra grasped the bed-post and hauled herself to her feet.

More soughing in her ears—and something rattled under her heel. A wave of desolation swept over her. It was Echo's water bowl.

"Oh, Echo," she said. "Please come back to me. *Please*." But she felt in her heart that Echo was far away.

It took ages to pull on her tunic, leggings, and boots, and as she did, snatches of memory returned. Userref holding her down while she thrashed with fever, and barking orders at Silea with uncharacteristic harshness. "What are you waiting for, girl? She needs water!"

"I *c-can't*," stammered Silea. "If I touch her, I'll die!"

Userref had sworn at the slave girl in Egyptian—something Pirra had never heard him do—then ordered her to go and fetch wood for the fire.

After she'd gone, he'd dripped ice water into Pirra's scorching mouth. "Pirra, can you hear me? I have to fetch dittany, it's the only thing that'll save you. There's none in the village, I'll be gone some time. I'll be back as soon as I can—"

"Userref, wait!" With feverish strength she'd clutched his wrist. "If I die—"

"You won't die," he'd cut in.

"*Listen* to me, you must hear this! The dagger of Koronos—"

"Pirra, hush—"

"I took it! On Thalakrea. I brought it to Keftiu."

"That's the fever talking—"

"It's *true*! I swear by the Eye of *Heru* . . ." Still clutching his wrist, she'd raised herself on one elbow. "If I die, *fetch* it. Take it somewhere the Crows can't find it. Guard it with your *life*, Userref—then destroy it!"

"You won't die," he'd repeated fiercely.

"*Swear*. That's an order."

At last it had dawned on him that she was telling the truth. Astonishment and even pride had flitted across his face; then he'd grasped his eye amulet and taken his oath.

Just before she'd slid back into the fever, she'd told him where the dagger was hidden. "Remember," she'd gasped, "it can only be destroyed by a god . . ."

Beyond the sanctuary walls, the waterfall thundered, but inside, all was deathly still. Wrapping her fox-fur cloak around her, Pirra groped to the door of her chamber.

The shrine was in darkness. As she padded past, she felt the Watchers following her with blind bronze eyes.

Userref's chamber was also empty and dark. She began to be uneasy. He should be back by now. Had something happened to him?

Silea's chamber too was dark and cold.

"Oh, you *wretch*," muttered Pirra. "If you're in the guardhouse again . . . Silea? Silea!" That ended in a fit of coughing. She decided that scolding could wait, she needed water.

All the jugs were empty. Cursing Silea, Pirra went back to the slave girl's chamber and kicked aside the mat that covered the hatch to the cellar, then climbed shakily down the ladder into the freezing, dank, earth-smelling dark.

Water gurgled in the pipe that led from the stream to the cistern. Fumbling for the rope, she hauled up the pail, a feat that left her sweating and floppy. The icy springwater set her teeth on edge, but the strength of Taka Zimi coursed through her. She found a sack of almonds and crammed a handful in her mouth, then some dried figs from a basket. Clutching more figs, she struggled up the ladder.

As an offering, she left one fig in the shrine. Munching the rest, she went out onto the steps.

It was night, and except for the dim snowglow, the courtyard was dark. The only sounds were the muffled thunder of the waterfall and the stream rushing past the walls.

A crow lit onto one of the bull's horns and cawed at her.

"Go 'way," she cried. The crow flew off; but her voice sounded reedy, and the stillness seemed deeper than before.

Pirra blinked.

*The courtyard was dark.* No torches on the walls. *No torches—no guards.*

A terrifying thought occurred to her. She hurried across the courtyard. The guardhouse door creaked as she pushed it open, and she felt the dead chill of a place that has stood empty for some time.

She ran to the gates. They were barred. "Let me out!"

she shouted. *Out, out* . . . The walls flung back her words. She tried to lift the crossbeam, but it took two strong men to do that: impossible for one fever-weakened girl.

In disbelief she blinked at the mess of footprints near the gates. Whoever had barred them had then climbed over them and pulled up the ladder, leaving her inside.

The crow returned, mocking her with harsh laughter. Still laughing, it flew off into the night.

Slowly, Pirra crossed the courtyard and climbed the steps. She stared at what she'd missed before. Chalked on the door of her chamber was a white handprint: *Plague*.

Silea and the guards had fled Taka Zimi. They had sealed her inside so that her ghost couldn't come after them—and left her for dead.

# 14

Hylas watched a crow fly past, and wondered if it was an omen. Since leaving the hut, he'd been nagged by a feeling that bad things were afoot on Mount Dikti.

All afternoon he'd been following Akastos' directions, climbing the ridge through the snowbound forest. He'd found the lightning-struck pine, but the clouds had closed in, and he could see no cloven crag or waterfall. Where was Taka Zimi?

And he was worried about Havoc. He'd last seen her when he'd collapsed outside the hut, and since then he'd found no tracks. Had she survived the blizzard? Would he ever see her again?

Ahead of him, a falcon swooped down to attack the crow. The falcon didn't seem to have noticed that the crow was a fledgling, and its parents were rushing to its defense. Now they were mobbing the would-be hunter with a furious onslaught of beaks and claws. The startled falcon took refuge in a pine tree, and the crows flew off with indignant caws.

Hylas peered up at the falcon, who huddled on a

branch, wide-eyed and gaping with alarm. He could tell from her speckled plumage that she was young. "That'll teach you to attack crows," he told her drily. "Next time, try pigeons."

Shaking out her feathers, the falcon flew off with a ringing *eck-eck eck*.

As Hylas watched her go, he thought of Pirra's sealstone, with its tiny engraved falcon. He remembered her fierce need for freedom, and his spirits plunged. He was no closer to finding her *or* Havoc.

*Where* was Taka Zimi?

The falcon was furious with herself. She'd failed *again*— and was reduced to scavenging a pitiful scrap of rotten hare that she'd found on a crag. When was she going to make a kill?

She missed the girl too. This was odd. After all, the girl was earthbound and human. But the falcon still missed her. She missed the girl's brilliant colors and her soft, slow breath. She missed the food she carried at her hip. Above all, she missed the way that when she flew, the girl's spirit seemed to fly with her.

Lifting onto the Wind, the falcon wheeled across the mountainside. Far below, she saw a vole burrowing in the snow and a boy toiling along a ridge. Up ahead, she glimpsed the eyrie with the juniper tree where she'd gotten stuck.

Suddenly, the falcon faltered in her flight. Something

was wrong. She didn't know what, but she felt it to the roots of her feathers.

Something to do with the girl.

The trees thinned and the ground fell away in a dizzying drop. Hylas' heart sank. *Stay as high as you can for as long as you can and avoid the gorge,* Akastos had warned. But here was the gorge yawning before him.

Three ropes had been strung across it. People made bridges like this back on Mount Lykas: one rope to stand on, and two at shoulder height to hold on to. Hylas hadn't trusted them then and he wasn't going to now. He must have left the ridge too soon. He had to go back and climb even higher.

He hadn't been long on the ridge when the clouds parted, and he saw a sheer crag of naked gray stone towering over him. It was cloven in two, and though he couldn't see the waterfall, he could hear its muffled roar. He quickened his pace. He still couldn't see Taka Zimi itself, but he knew he had found it.

A few paces on, he came to a line of big round paw prints in the snow. His belly turned over. Havoc's tracks were spattered with blood. Nightmare images flashed through his mind. Havoc gored by a bull or speared by a hunter . . .

The blood in the prints hadn't had time to freeze, which meant they were fresh. They led down to a clump of huge boulders on the eastern slope of the ridge.

Hylas hesitated. Should he track Havoc, or continue to Taka Zimi? Havoc or Pirra?

"Both," he said out loud. But it had to be Havoc first. Those tracks zigzagged, as if she'd been staggering, and the print of her left forepaw blurred: she'd been dragging her leg.

Dreading what he might find, Hylas followed the trail to a low cave hidden among the boulders. No tracks led out. Havoc was still inside.

"Havoc?" he called softly.

Silence. Snow fell from a branch, making him jump. He drew his knife. A wounded lion is one of the most dangerous creatures you can meet. And he wasn't even sure if Havoc had recognized him, let alone remembered that they'd once been friends.

Then it occurred to him that she would be wary of weapons. If she saw his knife, he wouldn't stand a chance. Shakily, he untied the sheath from his belt and set it in the snow by the cave mouth, along with his axe. What he was about to do was mad. It might be the last mistake he would ever make. But he couldn't abandon Havoc. Not again.

Dropping to his knees, he crawled inside the cave.

A deep, shuddering growl warned him back.

———

The lion cub lashed her tail and hissed—but the boy crawled *closer*. He was talking to her. She heard the fear in his voice and smelled it on his flesh, but still he came on.

Again she bared her teeth and hissed. *Go away!*

The boy halted. But he went on talking.

The pain bit her shoulder, and she panted and clawed the earth. The boy went on talking.

She would never trust a human again—and yet for the twitch of a tail, she remembered how he'd talked to her long ago, when she was little. His voice was deeper now, but it had the same gentleness and strength, and he was making the same sound he used to make when he called to her. Was it possible that he'd come to find her?

Again pain savaged her flesh, and she raked the earth with her claws.

The boy edged closer. His voice shook, but he kept talking.

Pain, fear, and hope fought within her. Surely he was just another human like all the rest . . .

Baring her teeth, she snarled at him. *Go—or I will strike!*

---

Hylas halted. Havoc's furious snarls filled the cave.

In the gloom, he saw the arrow shaft jutting from her shoulder. "Who shot you, Havoc?" he said as steadily as he could.

Havoc flattened her ears and gave him a murderous stare. Her eyes were black and cold. No trace of recognition.

"But you do remember me, don't you?" he faltered. "That's why you led me to Akastos in the blizzard. That's why you came and sniffed my face . . ."

Her throaty hiss blasted him back, and he caught the gleam of her huge white fangs.

Flattening himself against the cave wall so that she wouldn't feel trapped, he edged toward her. "Remember when you were a cub, and I made that wicker ball? And— when I pulled that thorn from your pad?"

Quicker than lightning, she lashed out with one paw, swiping the air a finger's-breadth from his cheek.

Sweat streamed down his flanks. "It hurt when I pulled out the thorn—but I made it better. Didn't I, Havoc?"

He was so close that he caught her musty lion smell and the coppery tang of blood. He saw her huge black claws flex in and out. One strike and she would snap his neck.

"B-but you don't want to hurt me, do you, Havoc?" he stammered.

With horrifying speed she lunged at him, clashing her fangs a whisker from his face.

"You d-don't want to hurt me," he repeated. "I'm your friend, I want to help."

For a moment they locked gazes. It was too dark to see if memories stirred in those slitted, pain-crazed eyes.

Hylas took a breath. He stretched one trembling hand toward the arrow shaft . . .

Then everything happened at once. He grabbed the shaft and pulled. Havoc's forepaw lashed out. Pain flared in his side as she flung him against the wall and sped from the cave.

The silence after she'd gone was deafening.

Wincing, Hylas probed his ribs. Sore, but not broken. Havoc had sheathed her claws. If she hadn't, she would have ripped him open from heart to hip.

Dazed and shaken, Hylas crawled to the mouth of the cave. He could see no sign of Havoc on the slope, apart from her blood-spattered trail disappearing into the trees. Would her wound heal? Would she understand that he'd done it to help her?

As his heartbeats slowed, he realized that he was still clutching the arrow.

He blinked at it. The arrowhead was shaped like a poplar leaf, and made of black obsidian.

His blood roared in his ears. Obsidian, like the arrowhead he had once dug out of his arm.

This could only mean one thing.

*Crows.*

# 15

From the lookout post on the wall, Pirra caught movement farther down the mountain. There among the pines: black cloaks and bronze spears. *Crows.*

Her mind darted in panic. They had tracked her here and were coming for the dagger. They would force their way in, and when they discovered that she didn't have it, they would torture her till she told them where it was.

Unless—unless they thought she had gone.

Crouching behind the juniper tree, she tore off her belt, leaned over the precipice, and tossed it onto a thorn bush. The lambskin snagged, as she'd hoped it would. Maybe the Crows would think she'd fallen.

Or maybe they would see through the trick in a heartbeat, and ransack Taka Zimi.

Scrambling down into the courtyard, she raced unsteadily for the sanctuary. She halted on the steps, straining to hear over the noise of the stream and her own panting breath.

She caught the distant crunch of boots in snow. *Already?*

She glanced over her shoulder. No no no. Her tracks cut across the courtyard like an arrow, pointing to where she'd gone. Biting her lips, she flew down and swept the snow with her cloak.

Harsh cries of men beyond the walls, a savage pounding at the gates. Pirra couldn't move, couldn't take her eyes from the crossbeam. It held—but it wouldn't keep them out for long.

Abruptly, the noises ceased. The silence was terrible. Then something heavy struck the top of the wall. Pirra's heart jerked. They had flung a rope around one of the bull's horns. Any moment now, a warrior would appear at the top and see her.

Nowhere to hide in her chamber. She darted for Silea's, kicked aside the mat, and yanked open the hatch to the cellar.

Your tracks! Again she retraced her steps, wiping her wet boot-prints off the stones. Then she half fell, half slid down the ladder into the cellar and paused at the bottom to listen.

Nothing. But she pictured warriors swarming over the walls, then lifting the crossbeam and letting in a black flood of Crows.

Soundlessly she lowered the hatch, struggling to keep hold of a corner of the mat, in a desperate attempt to conceal her hiding place. The darkness was so thick she couldn't see her hand before her face, but she found a gap behind an oil jar and squeezed behind it.

She smelled wet earth and heard the gurgle of the stream. Icy air blew through the hole she'd pecked away at over the winter. Waste of time. Earlier, when she'd realized that she'd been left for dead, she'd come down here and tried to enlarge it. She'd been so weak from the fever that she'd had to stop and crawl back to her bed to rest.

"Search everywhere, leave nothing intact," shouted a harsh voice that was dreadfully familiar.

Pirra's mind flew to last summer, when she'd faced Kreon in his stronghold. She remembered his greasy warrior braids and his massive fist crushing a harmless grass snake and flinging it writhing on the fire . . .

Clutching her sealstone, she tried to feel its tiny falcon. Her fingers were shaking too hard, she couldn't make it out.

As Telamon stood in the courtyard watching his men search the guardhouse, a falcon lit onto a juniper tree on the wall, uttering shrill cries of alarm.

The men stared at it. Kreon narrowed his eyes and fingered the bow slung over his shoulder. "A falcon," he muttered. "What does that mean?"

"It means she's here," said Telamon. "There's a falcon on her sealstone. It won't be long now."

Ilarkos ran over to them. "We found this," he panted, "snagged in a bush on the edge of that precipice."

Telamon took it without a word. It was a lambskin belt, intricately braided and gilded, as befitted Yassassara's daughter.

"She could have fallen," said Ilarkos. "Or jumped—"

"Or it's a trick," cut in Kreon.

Again the falcon uttered its *eck-eck* cries. Ilarkos cast it an uneasy glance. "Keftian magic is strong, my lord. They say their priestesses can turn themselves into birds . . ."

"She's not a priestess," Telamon said coldly as he wound the belt around his wrist. "She's just a girl."

"We've still got to find her," growled Kreon. "I'll take some men and search the slopes."

Telamon nodded. "I'll stay here and make sure they turn over every stone in this sanctuary. Don't worry, Uncle. We'll find her and we'll find the dagger."

"Let's hope so," Kreon said grimly.

But it wasn't only Ilarkos who was wary of Keftian magic; Telamon was annoyed to see that his men hadn't dared approach the sacred buildings.

To show them he wasn't afraid, he took the steps two at a time. He hesitated. Someone had chalked a Plague mark on the first door. If he entered that room, he might catch the Plague.

That's what the men are for, he told himself. I'm a leader. Leaders don't risk their lives for something like this.

Swiftly, he rubbed off the mark with his sleeve, then called to his men to search the room. The remaining doors were unmarked; he would deal with those himself.

As he entered the first, he reflected that something about that belt didn't feel right. Pirra hadn't jumped or fallen down that precipice. She was still here.

Pirra heard a man stride into the room above her head—and shrank deeper behind the oil jar.

A deafening crash made her start, and she nearly knocked over the jar. Silently, she begged the Goddess to stop the Crows from spotting the hatch.

More crashes and thuds. It sounded as if they were over-turning Silea's bed and smashing pots, lamps, everything. And still the hatch remained shut. Perhaps Silea's bed had fallen across it, hiding it from view.

Dust sifted onto Pirra's face, and she fought the urge to cough.

"I know you're here," said a voice above her, terrifyingly close.

She stopped breathing. She knew that voice.

"If you come out of your own accord," said Telamon, "we won't hurt you. I give you my word."

To her horror, she felt the beginnings of a sneeze. Clamping her hand over her mouth, she squeezed the bridge of her nose.

No sound from above. Telamon was listening.

The sneeze subsided. Shakily, she took away her hand. Her sweaty fingers found the sealstone at her wrist, and as she clutched the amethyst falcon, she prayed to the Goddess. *Hide me please please . . .*

The noise of running feet, and now another man was talking in an urgent murmur that she couldn't make out.

"Good," snapped Telamon. "Go and tell the lord Kreon."

Pirra's grip tightened on her sealstone. The tiny falcon dug into her palm.

"Pirra," said Telamon calmly. "I know you're here. My men searched your room. Your bed is still warm."

—⁂—

Riding the Wind, the falcon glanced down at the humans crawling like ants all over the eyrie. She couldn't see the girl, but she knew she was in trouble; she felt her call.

To get a closer look, the falcon tilted one wing and swooped toward the biggest of the humans. He was huge and lumbering, with weird black wings hanging limp and flightless down his back, like a crow's, only without the purple and green. She caught his bitter stink and sensed his rage—and also his fear.

He seemed to be frightened of her. As she swept over his head, he ducked. The falcon was astonished. Did he imagine she was stupid enough to hit him? He was enormous; she'd rather crash into a boulder. But the human didn't seem to realize that, and this gave the falcon an idea.

When she swooped again, the human bent back a stick and sent another stick wobbling through the air toward her. This stick was so ridiculously slow that she dodged it with scornful ease. Did he think he could hit a falcon with that?

Letting the Wind carry her out of reach, she scanned the mountainside. She saw more crow-men floundering in the snow below the eyrie. She caught the purple flash of a weasel near the rainbow torrent of the waterfall. *But where was the girl?*

At that moment, the falcon spotted movement in the bushes below the waterfall. It was that boy again, the one who'd watched her failing to kill a crow.

The falcon flew nearer.

This boy wasn't one of the crow-men. He smelled of the forest, and he puzzled her, because unlike all the other humans the falcon had ever seen, his hair wasn't black; it was dark gold with flashes of red, like an eagle.

---

From his hiding place below the waterfall, Hylas watched in horror as the Crows ransacked Taka Zimi: hauling chests onto the steps and hacking them to pieces with axes, spearing mattresses and smashing stools, pots, lamps.

He could see no sign of Pirra, and it flashed across his mind that such savagery might mean that they *hadn't* found her, and were venting their rage.

Suddenly he caught movement above, and a bird swept overhead. It was that falcon again, the young one he'd seen being mobbed by crows. Puzzled, he watched her wheeling over Taka Zimi, shrieking her alarm call at the warriors.

This had to be a sign. *She's still here,* the bird's shrill cries seemed to be saying. *She needs your help.*

At least—Hylas thought that was what it meant. If he was wrong, he was about to risk his life for nothing.

From his hiding place, the stream tumbled down a scree

slope dotted with juniper bushes, and rushed past a corner of the sanctuary. There wasn't much cover, although at least the water might mask the sound of his approach.

And then what? Those walls were unclimbable, and the whole place was crawling with Crows.

As Hylas hesitated, he caught a bitter tang on the wind, and his belly tightened. Black smoke was rising from the roof of the sanctuary, and orange flames were flaring in the thatch.

If Pirra was inside, her time was running out.

The Crows were setting Taka Zimi on fire.

# 16

The crackle of flames grew louder, and smoke seeped into the cellar. Pirra's heart hammered in her chest. If she stayed down here, she would die.

The hatch above her head felt hot, and when she pushed, it didn't budge. She pushed harder. No use. She fought the urge to scream. She'd prayed to the Goddess to hide her—but whatever concealed the hatch was now shutting her in.

"Pirra, it's over!" Telamon's voice was muffled; he must have fled to the courtyard. "Tell me where you are and I'll save you!"

Pirra pictured him standing triumphant in the snow—and her panic turned to cold hard rage. *You'd like that, wouldn't you, Telamon? Then you could show me off as your captive and make all Keftiu bow before you. Well, I'm not some weasel in a hole, I'm the daughter of Yassassara—and I beg no man for help.*

"Pirra, come out!" yelled Telamon. "It's not worth dying!"

Gritting her teeth, Pirra groped for the hammer and

wedge she'd hidden near the water pipe. She would make one last attempt to dig herself out. She'd rather die trying than give in to the Crows.

The wedge was where she'd left it, stuck in the joint between two stones edging the hole. She hit the wedge as hard as she could, and one of the stones rocked. She struck again and again—kicked, pulled, hammered. Couldn't work it free.

"Pirra, this is madness!" shouted Telamon.

With rising panic, she kept going. Suddenly the stone moved by itself. Then someone yanked it out, a hand reached through and grabbed her wrist, and she heard a hoarse whisper. "Pirra! It's me!"

⸻

To Hylas' relief, Pirra didn't waste an instant asking how he'd found her. The Crows might appear at any moment.

The first stone had doubled the size of the hole, which made it easier to get at the next. In frantic silence they attacked it together, Hylas digging and levering with a stick, Pirra hammering from inside. At last the stone jolted free. With both feet, Hylas kicked in another one—and before he could help her, she'd wriggled through.

Seizing her hand, he half dragged her up the slope. The wind helped, hiding them in choking smoke as they scrambled from bush to bush. But it would hide the Crows too.

At last they reached the boulders below the waterfall, where Hylas had hidden to spy out the sanctuary. Pirra leaned against a rock, bent double, with her hands on her knees. For the first time, he got a good look at her. He was shocked. Her face was gray and painfully thin, with dark-blue shadows under her eyes. She didn't look strong enough to make it up to the ridge, let alone trek across a mountain.

"Are you all right?" he panted.

"No," she snapped, suddenly a lot more like herself. "I've had fever, I'm weak as a cat. And I've lost my sealstone," she added, staring in horror at a bloody scratch on her wrist.

He snorted. "Well, you can't go back for it now."

"I know that," she retorted.

He flashed her a grin—which she didn't return. It was taking all her resolve just to stay standing.

Below them, the roof of Taka Zimi collapsed with a crash, and orange flames shot skyward. Through the smoke, Hylas glimpsed warriors searching the ground near the walls. Soon they would find Pirra's escape hole and pick up their trail.

Hylas thought fast. Returning the way he'd come would mean a long, steep climb past the waterfall and onto the ridge. Even if Pirra managed it, she'd never outrun the Crows. There had to be another way . . .

"Let's go," he said. "If we head down the other side of this slope, we'll come to a gorge. There's a bridge. When we're across, we'll cut it; that'll give us a good day's lead."

Under cover of the smoke, they started off, stumbling between the pines toward where Hylas reckoned the gorge must be—although in this smoke, it was hard to tell. Trees and boulders loomed out of the haze, but no Crow warriors. Which didn't mean they weren't close behind.

To his relief, the pines thinned—and there was the gorge, with the bridge just a few paces away.

"That's not a bridge," panted Pirra, "that's a rope!"

"It's a bridge," said Hylas. "One for the feet, two for the hands. But we need to go barefoot." Already he was yanking off his boots and tying them around his neck.

"I can't do it," she said. "I—"

"You can. Quick, take off your boots and tie them round your neck."

After an instant's hesitation, she did, although he could see that she didn't think she'd make it across.

"The trick is to keep moving," he told her, "but don't rush and *don't* look down."

The "bridge" was braided rawhide, lashed on this side to three wind-battered pines and on the other to a clump of sturdy oaks. It was maybe twenty paces long, and the drop to the bottom was stomach-churning. One wrong move and they'd be splattered all over the rocks.

"Will it take both our weights?" muttered Pirra.

"Yes," said Hylas, although he was far from sure. Blessing Periphas for his gift of rope, he tied one end around his waist and the other around Pirra's, leaving a couple of arm-spans' slack between, so they could move independently.

Pirra was shaking her head. "If we're tied together and I fall, I'll take you with me."

"No you won't, I'll hang on somehow."

To prevent further protest, he grasped both hand ropes

at shoulder height and stepped onto the footrope. All three were strung so taut that they barely sagged: thank the gods that these Keftians knew what they were doing.

"Keep your eyes on me," he said over his shoulder, "and *don't look down*."

---

The bridge held firm, but swayed alarmingly in the wind gusting up from below, and behind him Pirra wobbled so badly that she nearly tipped them both upside down. Somehow, they managed to keep going, and the oaks on the other side drew nearer.

Once, Hylas glanced around. Pirra's face was set, and she was staring fixedly over his shoulder. He didn't speak in case he put her off.

They were a few paces from safety when shouts rang out behind, and an arrow hissed past Hylas' ear. His mind reeled. High above the gorge, they were easy targets. Or maybe the Crows would cut the ropes and send them plummeting to their deaths.

The same thought had occurred to Pirra; the rope around his waist jerked as she halted, and he fought to stay upright. "Keep moving!" he told her. "We're nearly there!"

"It's no use running, Hylas!" shouted a voice behind him.

Now it was Hylas who lurched. That voice was Telamon's.

Over Pirra's head, Hylas glimpsed his erstwhile friend at the edge of the gorge, nocking another arrow to his bow.

Warriors ran up to support him. Hylas quickened his pace, hating the fact that Pirra was behind him and he could do nothing to shield her from their arrows.

One struck an oak directly ahead; more bounced off the rocks. Hylas leaped for solid ground—staggered—then grabbed a branch of the oak and spun around to hold Pirra if she fell.

She was nearly at the edge, but now on the far side, Hylas saw Telamon shoulder his bow and start across the bridge. Hylas whipped out his axe to cut the footrope—but Pirra was still on it. "*Hurry!*" he urged her.

Her foot slipped. He pulled the rope taut about her waist as she fought to steady herself.

The wind whipped Telamon's long dark hair about his face, but still he came on. Then Kreon—*Kreon,* the tyrant of Thalakrea—moved right to the edge and drew back his bowstring to take aim at Pirra.

Suddenly a dark bolt hurtled out of the clouds and swept past Kreon's head. The Crow Chieftain faltered. So did Pirra. "*Echo,*" she cried. "You came back!"

"Pirra, *come on!*" yelled Hylas.

The next instant she staggered to safety—and Hylas brought down his axe on the footrope.

The rawhide resisted, but Telamon lurched and nearly fell.

"Telamon, turn back and get off the bridge!" warned Hylas. "I don't want to kill you, but I will if you take another step!"

Telamon took another step.

Hylas hacked at the rope. Telamon's face worked in fury, but he saw that Hylas meant it, and made his way back to solid ground. A heartbeat later, Hylas struck the rope and it snapped. With Crow arrows hissing and clattering around him, he used the oaks for cover and cut one of the hand ropes, then ran to help Pirra, who was sawing at the other with her knife.

On the far side of the gorge, Telamon lifted his sword to the sky. "You can't get away from me, Outsider!" he roared, his face twisted with rage. "I swear by the Angry Ones and by the dagger of Koronos that I will hunt you down, I will feed your carcass to the dogs!"

For a moment they faced each other across the void. Then Hylas cut the last rope and sent it hurtling into the gorge.

# 17

"Wait," panted Pirra, "I have to rest."

"Just for a bit," said Hylas. "Dark soon, we've got to find shelter."

Wearily, she slumped onto a rock. Hylas was alarmed to see that her lips were tinged with blue. She couldn't go much farther.

They hadn't spoken since leaving the gorge. It had taken all their strength to scramble over boulder-strewn slopes and through snowbound forests, and now they were at the bottom of a wooded gully. Silent firs guarded a frozen stream, and the slopes were pocked with the dark mouths of caves.

There'd been no sign of the Crows, and Hylas guessed they must be at least a day behind. Unless of course they'd found another way down.

Leaning against a tree, he waited for Pirra to recover. She sat in a cloud of frosty breath, clutching her knees. They glanced at each other, then swiftly away, both aware of the months they'd spent apart and the weight of things unsaid.

"Better be going," said Hylas.

Raising her head, Pirra gave him a level stare. "What are you doing on Keftiu? Why did you come and find me?"

"Pirra, not here, there isn't time—"

"I need to know."

There was too much to say and he didn't know how, so instead he said, "Why are the Crows after you?"

She licked her lips. "They think I've got the dagger," she said under her breath.

"*What*? But—I thought *they* did."

She shook her head. "I brought it to Keftiu."

He stared at her. "So—on Thalakrea when I put you on that ship—"

"Yes. I had it then."

"Where is it now?"

"I hid it."

"Where?"

She glanced over her shoulder. "Do you really want me to tell you out here in the open, where anyone might be listening?"

She was right and he didn't press her; but as they headed off, he struggled to take it in.

Night gathered under the trees, and he started looking for a campsite. Pirra kept glancing expectantly at the sky, as if she was waiting for something to appear. He spotted a cave that might do. Telling her to wait, he climbed up to check it for bears.

At first the cave appeared promising, but as he crawled

deeper, he felt the warning ache in his temple. At the corner of his vision, he glimpsed a shadowy man and woman. Their breath didn't smoke—because they *had* no breath—and around them swarmed a seething mass of Plague.

"That one's no good," he told Pirra as he ran down to her. "We'll have to keep looking."

"What's wrong with it? You've gone pale—"

"It's nothing, it's—it wasn't right."

She shot him a puzzled glance, but didn't ask any more. Then she saw something over his shoulder and her face lit up. "*Echo!*" she cried. "You came back! You came back!"

Farther down the gully, Hylas made out the young falcon, perched on a rock by a clump of junipers.

"Echo!" Pirra called softly—and to Hylas' astonishment, the bird flew to her and landed on her wrist. "I kept calling her in my mind," she told him. "I felt that she was coming, but I didn't know when. And look, she's found another cave." She pointed to a patch of darkness behind the boulder that had been the falcon's perch.

"How do we know it's all right?" said Hylas.

"If Echo thinks it's all right," said Pirra with startling confidence, "then it is."

⸻

The cave turned out to be perfect: hidden and dry, with a fissure at the back, which meant they could risk a small fire. Hylas went to gather wood, and Pirra crawled inside and slumped with her head on her knees.

She was dizzy with fatigue and still shaky from the fever.

She was also confused. Now that Echo had returned and they seemed to be safe for a while, she could allow herself to think about Hylas. All through the winter she'd been furious with him, but now . . . she didn't know what to feel.

And she dreaded telling him about Havoc. How was she going to break the news that his beloved lion cub had been lost in the Great Wave?

As if sensing her confusion, Echo ran toward her, her talons clicking on the rocks. With her forefinger, Pirra stroked the falcon's scaly yellow foot. "I'm so glad you came back," she said softly. Echo took the toe of Pirra's boot in her beak and gave it a tug. Then she decided it wasn't worth eating and flew to the rock at the cave mouth, where she settled herself on one leg for a nap.

Pirra realized she was ravenous: She hadn't eaten since Taka Zimi. Rummaging in Hylas' food pouch, she found six wizened olives and a lump of sooty cheese the size of a goose's egg. She wolfed two olives, left three for him, and offered one to Echo—who just blinked at it, so Pirra ate it herself.

Hylas crawled in with an armful of firewood. Without looking at her, he started laying the fire. "Feeling better?" he said.

"Mm," she lied. "I ate some of the olives."

He nodded. "We'll split the rest when I've woken a fire. When the snow in the waterskin's melted, we'll have something to drink." He was talking too much. Pirra wondered if, like her, he didn't know what to say.

She watched him strike sparks between two stones in a handful of bark. A tiny red flame flared, and he bent and blew on it softly to make it grow.

He'd changed since last summer. He was taller, and his shoulders were broader. His voice was deeper, which made him seem different from the boy she had known, and in his rough sheepskins, he looked startlingly foreign: more Akean than when she'd last seen him.

"Did you find your sister?" she said awkwardly.

"No," he said, snapping sticks over his knee. "I heard—I heard your mother died. I'm sorry."

"I don't want to talk about it," she said curtly.

"Right."

She was almost disappointed that he took her at her word. The harder she tried not to think about her mother, the more she did. Her feelings were a painful tangle of anger and loss. She wished Hylas would help her sort it out.

On her perch, Echo stretched out one wing and began preening with furious little beak-clickings.

"Does she need water?" Hylas said suddenly.

"She needs meat, but I don't think she knows how to hunt."

"She doesn't. I saw her chase a baby crow and get mobbed by its parents."

They exchanged tentative smiles.

Hylas described how he'd seen Echo wheeling over Taka Zimi. "That's how I knew you were there."

Pirra went to the falcon and put out her finger. "Thank

you, Echo," she said. Echo gave her finger a gentle peck, then went back to tidying her feathers.

The fire crackled and warmth stole through the cave. They shared the cheese, and Hylas put a crumb at the foot of Echo's rock. The falcon shot him a wary glance, then surprised Pirra by hopping down and eating it.

"I didn't even know she liked cheese," said Pirra with a twinge of jealousy.

"Tomorrow I'll see if I can catch her a mouse," said Hylas. He asked how she'd met Echo, and she told him. Then she asked how he'd survived since Thalakrea, and he told her about roaming the Sea with a gang of escaped slaves.

"Do you miss them?" she said.

"I miss Periphas. But sometimes when I was with him, I almost forgot about Issi and you and Havoc. I hated that."

At the mention of Havoc, Pirra's belly turned over. "Hylas . . ." she faltered. "About Havoc—"

"I wish she was here now. The last time I saw her was on the other side of the mountain, and—"

"She's *alive?*" cried Pirra, startling Echo. "I thought she'd drowned in the Great Wave!"

"It's because of Havoc I knew about the Crows," said Hylas. "I pulled one of their arrows out of her shoulder."

"They shot her? Is she all right?"

"I don't know. I wish I did."

At the thought of the Crows, they fell silent, listening to the firs moaning in the night wind. In her head, Pirra saw Kreon's murderous glare as he took aim at her with his bow. She heard Telamon screaming his oath to hunt Hylas to the death.

"Do you miss your sealstone?" said Hylas, startling her. "You keep rubbing your wrist."

"Oh. Well, I've had it since I was born, so it feels weird without it."

She asked if he still had the lion claw she'd given him, and he drew it out on a thong from the neck of his jerkin. Then he asked if she had the knife he'd made for her.

"Um. No," she said. "I chucked it overboard as the ship left Thalakrea."

"Ah," said Hylas.

"I threw away your falcon feather too." She flicked him a glance. "Seven moons, Hylas. Seven moons shut up at Taka Zimi—because of you."

He sat with his arms about his knees, scowling at the flames. Firelight glinted in his fair hair and lit the strong, bony planes of his face. "The last thing you said to me on Thalakrea," he said, "is that you'd hate me forever."

"You'd just bundled me onto a ship and sent me back to captivity."

"I was trying to save you."

"You didn't give me a choice, you decided for me."

"There was no time! And when I put you on that ship, I had no idea Keftiu would suffer worst of all. I didn't know the Great Wave was going to happen, or the Plague." He paused. "But you're right. It's my fault you were shut up at Taka Zimi. I'm sorry."

Pirra stared at her boots. "Well, if it wasn't for you, I'd have burned to death or been caught by the Crows, so I'm glad you found me."

She glanced up to find him watching her with an unreadable expression in his tawny eyes. "It's good to see you, Pirra," he said quietly.

She flushed. "Is it?"

"Yes. It really is."

Her flush deepened, and she sucked in her lips. "Well. It's good to see you too."

Another silence.

A beetle had wobbled its way to the end of a stick and was in danger of falling into the fire. Hylas picked it up and set it down at a safe distance. Then he went off, muttering about fetching fir branches to sleep on.

As Pirra waited for him to return, the warmth of the fire made her sleepy, and her thoughts began to blur. She seemed to be back in the cellar, with the flames crackling overhead and smoke seeping through the hatch . . .

She jolted awake. "Userref!" she cried.

Echo squawked, and Hylas came running. "What's wrong!"

"I just realized! Userref—he'll find Taka Zimi in ruins, he'll think I'm dead!"

Hylas looked puzzled. "But you're not, so what does it—"

"No, you don't understand! When I was ill, I made him swear that if I died, he would fetch the dagger and destroy it. So now . . . oh, poor Userref." She pictured the Egyptian staring in horror at the smoking ruins of Taka Zimi. He would be devastated. He had devoted his whole life to keeping her safe.

"Pirra?" said Hylas. "Did you hear what I said? The dagger. Where is it now?"

She swallowed. "I hid it. As soon as we got to Keftiu, I hid it, but then my mother sent me to Taka Zimi that same day and I didn't have a chance to take it with me—"

"So where is it?" he cut in.

"In the House of the Goddess."

—◦—

"The House of the Goddess," repeated Hylas. "Which is standing empty. Unguarded. The Crows could just walk in and take it."

"They'd never find it," said Pirra, "not if they searched for ten years. Besides, they don't know it's there, they think I've got it."

They fell silent, turning this over in their minds.

"We can't leave it there," said Hylas. "As long as it exists, it's a threat."

"I know. We have to get it before they do. We have to destroy it."

Yes, but how? thought Hylas. To destroy the dagger of Koronos was no easy thing. He remembered what Akastos had told him in the smithy on Thalakrea: *No forge made by mortal men will ever be hot enough to destroy it. The dagger of Koronos can only be destroyed by a god.*

And how, thought Hylas, are we to make that happen, when the gods have abandoned Keftiu?

"Of course," said Pirra, "if the Crows pick up our trail, we'll be leading them straight to it."

"I thought of that too," said Hylas. "But we'll have to risk it." Then he met her eyes. "Problem is, Pirra, how do we find the House of the Goddess? I've no idea where we are. Do you?"

# 18

Hylas dreamed about Issi, and woke with an ache in his chest.

It was still dark, and Pirra was fast asleep. Silently, he got ready to go hunting by masking his scent with woodash; then he took his slingshot and crept out into the snow.

The sky was beginning to lighten and the forest was waking up. A pine marten peered down at him from a fir, and a pair of jays chattered overhead. This told him that the Crows couldn't be close; otherwise, these creatures would have fled.

In the gray half-light, he spotted more signs of life: the knife-sharp pattern of an owl's wings where it had punched into the snow after a vole, and the tracks of a badger, like those of a small purposeful bear. But not the paw prints of a lion.

The ache in his chest sharpened. He missed Havoc. He missed her eager little grunts when she told him things in lion talk, and her determined, mostly doomed attempts to sneak up on him unawares. Somehow when she was with him, Issi didn't seem so far away, and he felt that if he could look after Havoc, the Lady of the Wild Things would watch over his sister.

His hunting luck was good, and he downed a hare nibbling willow bark, and two partridges. He set the hare's head in a tree as an offering for the god of Mount Dikti, left the paws for the Lady of the Wild Things, and on impulse, placed one of the partridges under a bush for Havoc.

He couldn't bear to think of her out here alone. If he didn't find her, she'd be on her own for the rest of her life. And that wouldn't last long. Lions need company, or they die.

"Havoc!" he called softly.

A weasel glanced at him as it flickered past, and a raven lit onto a branch with a sonorous *cark!*

"Havoc! Where *are* you?"

Snow sifted down as the raven hitched its wings and flew away.

---

"Havoc, where *are* you?"

Hylas' voice sounded rough with longing, and Pirra withdrew behind a boulder so that he wouldn't see her.

A bit later, she joined him. He was squatting in the snow, plucking a partridge. His face was open and raw, and she felt sorry for him.

"Sleep all right?" he said without raising his head.

She hesitated. She still felt a bit shaky, but she didn't want to go into that, so instead she asked if he'd seen Echo.

With his knife he pointed to a crag. "Up there, watching for prey."

Pirra peered at the falcon-shaped dot. Suddenly Echo bobbed her head a few times, then spread her wings and swept down the gully. Pirra felt a tug in her chest, and the painful sense that she could almost fly.

"Bad choice, Echo," murmured Hylas. "Don't go after magpies."

"What's wrong with magpies?" said Pirra.

"They're too clever, they know all the tricks."

Sure enough, the wily magpie sped straight for a patch of brambles and disappeared. Echo flew over it a couple of times, then realized it was hopeless, and returned to Pirra for reassurance.

"Better luck next time," Pirra told her soothingly. The falcon drew a lock of her hair through her bill, as if to preen.

"She should stick to pigeons," Hylas remarked.

He seemed to be feeling better, so Pirra asked him to show her how to use a slingshot. He gave in when she insisted, and back at the cave, while he butchered the hare, she loaded the slingshot with a pine cone and swung it over her head.

"Faster," said Hylas. "You only get to swing it a couple of times before the prey hears, so you have to be *fast*. Now let go of the knotted end and you'll hit that bush . . . Or not."

At the seventh attempt, she almost struck the bush, and

at the tenth, she nearly got Hylas. "How long is this going to take?" she complained.

"In your case I'd say months," he said drily. "Or I could just catch a squirrel and hold it down for you—"

Her snowball struck him smack in the chest. He chucked one back, and they forgot about the slingshot and pelted each other.

Suddenly, Hylas' face changed, and the snowball fell from his hand. Pirra glanced over her shoulder.

Havoc stood twenty paces away in a haze of frosty breath. She was much bigger and shaggier than when Pirra had last seen her, with a ridge of darker fur running from between her ears to her shoulder blades, like a full-grown lion. But her legs and paws were still spotted, and there was something cub-like about her face. Her large amber eyes were fixed on Hylas.

"*Havoc,*" he said.

The lion cub snuffed the air and made soft little *yowmp-yowmp* noises. In three bounds she was on him, flinging her forepaws around his shoulders in a powerful lion hug, and he was hugging her back and burying his face in her scruff, and they were rolling in the snow, so that Pirra could hardly tell boy from lion.

---

"I wonder how she survived the winter," said Pirra, licking hare grease off her fingers.

"Scavenging, probably," said Hylas. He'd given Havoc the hare's innards and ears, and was now feeding her the slippery marrow, which she loved just as much as when she was little.

"You don't think—she didn't eat *people*?" said Pirra.

"No," he said firmly. "Not Havoc."

Havoc got to her feet and rubbed her forehead against his, and he sank his hands into the deep hot fur of her flanks and scratched her hard, the way she loved, breathing in her musky lion smell.

*I'll never leave you again*, he told her silently.

Echo flew to Pirra and perched on her shoulder, and Pirra gave her the partridge wing she'd saved. Havoc saw the falcon and started purposefully toward her. Echo took fright and flew to a tree with her prize.

Pirra cast Hylas an anxious glance. "D'you think they'll get along?"

"Not sure," he said.

After erasing all trace of their camp, they set off. Their plan—such as it was—was to skirt the mountain's flank, then head north and *hope* to find the coast—and somewhere, the House of the Goddess.

They walked all day without incident, and camped for the night in another cave, sharing what was left of the partridge. After they'd eaten, Hylas sat whittling a fishhook from the hare's legbone, while Havoc lay against his thigh, quietly crunching the last of the partridge, held tight between her forepaws. Pirra curled on her side, gazing at the embers.

Echo perched on a rock beyond the cave mouth, one

eye shut, the other fixed warily on Havoc. All day, lion and falcon had maintained a prickly distance. Hylas wondered how long it would last.

He put another log on the fire, and Pirra narrowed her eyes against the light. As dusk had fallen, she'd turned quiet, rubbing her wrist where her sealstone used to be.

"Are you thinking about your mother?" Hylas said carefully.

"No," she said. But he could tell that she was.

"Were you with her when she died?"

"No," she said again. She chewed her lower lip. "A priest came and told me. He said she was going to do a Mystery—that's a secret rite—to bring back the Sun and rid Keftiu of Plague; but it got her first." Her dark brows drew together. "He said she was buried sitting up in her coffin, with a gold band around her head. It had eyes engraved on it. Wide staring eyes, so that she can watch over Keftiu forever . . ." She broke off. Hylas could see that she was struggling to hold back her feelings. She'd hated her mother, but she'd respected her too. Yassassara had been so strong, and now she was gone. The shock must run deep.

To change the subject, he said, "What did you do all winter at Taka Zimi?"

She made a face. "Walked round the courtyard and got bored. Learned some Egyptian with Userref and got bored. Squabbled with Silea, my slave girl, and—"

"Got bored," finished Hylas.

She snorted a laugh.

Echo awoke and turned her head right around to glare at Havoc, who pretended not to notice.

Pirra said, "Do you think she'll ever learn to hunt? Echo, I mean."

"In time," said Hylas. "But she needs to go after pigeons. And she needs to hunt into the wind."

"Why?"

"That's what falcons do. Their wings are stronger than the prey's, so the wind slows the prey down more than it does the falcon."

"How do you *know* all these things?"

He shrugged. "It's boring being a goatherd. Nothing to do except watch goats. If I hadn't watched other creatures, I'd have gone mad."

Again Pirra laughed.

After that there was a companionable silence, and a little later, Pirra rolled herself in her cloak and went to sleep.

Hylas sat on with Havoc. The lion cub had finished the partridge, and lay on her belly with one huge forepaw curled inside the other. Her face had lost that grim, taut look, and the wound in her shoulder was healing well.

Hylas scratched the pale fur under her chin, and she gazed up at him and rumbled happily. Over the winter, her large, slanted, black-rimmed eyes had darkened from the color of honey to the rich amber of beech leaves in autumn. She was going to be a beautiful lioness—and a powerful one. Although she wasn't yet full-grown, when she stood beside him, her head brushed his thigh, and she had at least five times his strength.

She yawned hugely, baring white fangs as long as his thumb, then rose, stretched, and rubbed her forehead against his.

I wish it was always like this, thought Hylas. Everyone together and safe. If Issi were here, it would be perfect.

When the lion cub awoke, it was the middle of the Dark. She lay contentedly snuffing the boy's warm foresty scent. Then she rolled over and flung one forepaw across his face to wake him up.

He mumbled and pushed her off, and she nosed his flank, but he went on sleeping. Such sleeps these humans had, she thought fondly. And always in the Darks, the best time to hunt!

The lion cub was *happy*. The boy *hadn't* abandoned her, he'd come all the way across the Great Gray Beast to find her. Now they would never be parted, not ever again.

Rising to her feet, she had a good long stretch, then padded over to the sleeping girl and gave her a light muzzle-rub, because she too was part of the pride.

On a rock near the mouth of the lair perched that falcon who'd taken to hanging about. The cub thought about taking a swipe at her, but the falcon guessed and flew to the top of a pine, where she sat glaring down at the cub. Twitching her tail, the cub glared back. Stay away. They're my humans.

Suddenly, the lion cub pricked her ears. The wind carried voices: stealthy and human. Flaring her nostrils, the cub picked up the scent she'd smelled before: the humans who'd been watching the pride all through the not-Light, although the boy and girl hadn't noticed.

The humans were easy to find in the Dark, two men crouching behind a rock a few bounds above the lair. They weren't the terrible men with the flapping black hides, but they were sneaky, and they worried the cub. What did they want?

Picking her way noiselessly between the pines, the lion cub climbed in a wide loop so that the sneaky humans wouldn't sense her, then belly-crawled closer.

When she was within an easy pounce, she snarled.

The men fled in terror, and she bounded after them— not to catch them, just to scare them into not coming back.

Then, when she was sure they were really gone, the lion cub trotted back to the lair and settled down to guard her humans.

# 19

"I still don't see," said Hylas as they struggled through yet another icy ravine, "how you could live your whole life in the House of the Goddess, but have no idea where it is."

"I *told* you," snarled Pirra, "they never let me out. All I know is it's about half a day's walk from the north coast—"

"You're sure that's north and not south," muttered Hylas.

She shot him a look, which he ignored. Pirra always got bad-tempered when she was thirsty.

It didn't help that Echo and Havoc weren't getting along. At first it had been hisses and glares, but then Hylas had shared a squirrel between them, and Echo had tried to steal Havoc's and the lion cub had taken a swipe at her, which the falcon had narrowly escaped.

To make matters worse, both were intensely jealous of any attention the other received from Hylas or Pirra. Earlier, Pirra had stroked Havoc, which had prompted Echo to fly off in a sulk; and when Pirra lured her down with a mouse Hylas had caught, *Havoc* had stalked off with wounded glances: *Why are you being nice to a* bird?

Now, as Hylas led the way between snow-covered boulders, he could feel Pirra brooding over what the cub might do to her beloved Echo. He worried about this himself. Until now, Havoc had been happily exploring the forest, often disappearing for long periods. What if he found her sitting under a tree with a mouthful of falcon feathers?

"Are we going in circles?" said Pirra, behind him.

"Of course not!" he said irritably. But after a day spent scrambling over ridges and detouring around unclimbable crags, he was starting to worry that they might be doing exactly that. And if it was true, the Crows could be anywhere.

Which, he had to admit, was hardly Pirra's fault. "Sorry," he mumbled over his shoulder.

She didn't reply.

"I said I'm sorry!" he snapped.

When she still didn't answer, he turned around.

Pirra wasn't there. In disbelief, Hylas took in rocks and juniper trees, and tracks in the snow that belonged to him alone.

"Pirra," he called, "if this is a joke, it's not funny."

But it didn't feel like a joke. Drawing his knife, he retraced his steps.

The ravine was narrow, and the junipers tall and dense. "Pirra?"

Strong hands grabbed him and yanked him into the dark.

In a heartbeat he was blindfolded, stripped of his gear, and his arms tied behind his back. Someone seized his hair and jerked his head back. He heard muttering and smelled the tang of dittany; he guessed that a wisewoman was checking him for signs of Plague.

They must have decided he didn't have it, because someone pushed his head down and steered him through an echoing space that felt like a cave. So far, his captors hadn't said a word, but he guessed they weren't Crows, or he'd have been dead by now.

The echoes changed and he sensed space opening around him. He smelled smoke and heard shuffling hooves, the huffing breath of livestock, and an angry murmur of voices. Then he was forced to sit on the ground and his blindfold was pulled off.

He was in a huge cavern, dimly lit by a smoky dung fire and thronged with goats, sheep, oxen, dogs, and people. He saw men with the weathered features and the crooked limbs of peasants, armed with scythes, pitchforks, and hostile expressions. Grimy women nursed babies and glared at him. Children gawped openmouthed; they had the same bizarrely shaven heads and single locks as the ghosts at the coast.

It flashed across his mind that at least Havoc and Echo were safe in the forest. Then he saw Pirra. She sat not far from him, bound, bedraggled, and furious. "Did they hurt you?" he said.

"No. You?"

He shook his head. "Who *are* these people?"

"Leave this to me, they don't speak Akean."

Their captors didn't like them talking in a tongue they couldn't understand, and a scrawny man at the front— Hylas guessed he was the leader—barked at Pirra in Keftian.

She spat a retort that drew sharp intakes of breath from the crowd, but the scrawny man merely snorted. Like all Keftian men, he had no beard; his mouth was puckered, as if he'd tasted something bad, and his small hot eyes glared at Pirra with startling bitterness.

At an order from him, a woman sullenly untied Pirra's wrists. Pirra scrambled to her feet and launched another tirade.

"Whatever you're saying, you're making it worse," muttered Hylas.

"I said leave it to me," she told him.

As he watched her berating their captors in her hawk-like tongue, he felt as if he was seeing her for the first time. Despite her small stature and filthy clothes, no one could doubt that she was the daughter of the High Priestess. Her imperious tone and upright carriage, even her crescent-moon scar, set her apart.

But he could tell that she was frightened.

---

"Who are you and how dare you treat me like this!" said Pirra with as much authority as she could muster.

"Hold your tongue!" snapped the woman who'd untied her.

"Hush, Tanagra," chided a burly man with a heavy brow and a squashed-looking nose. "That's no way to address the daughter of Yassassara."

"That's exactly how to talk to her, Deukaryo," cut in the scrawny leader. Then to Pirra, "You! Show some respect!"

"Who are you?" demanded Pirra.

"My name is Sidayo—and *I'm* leader here," he said with a glance at the burly Deukaryo. "I was a water-carrier in your mother's House, but I was born in Tusiti. Most of us are from Tusiti. We were fishermen and farmers. Now we live in the mountains and scrape an existence as herdsmen."

"Tusiti," said Pirra. "Isn't that on the coast?"

"It was," Sidayo said bitterly. "When it still existed. Before the Wave."

"We worshipped the Sea," put in the woman, Tanagra, "because the priests told us to. Now we can't bear to be anywhere near it. That's why we fled. We're never going back."

"The Sea took everything," said Sidayo. "It drowned our village and rotted our crops. Smashed our boats, tore the clothes off our backs. We had to strip *corpses* to get something to wear."

"It took my children," Tanagra said fiercely. "It didn't even leave me their bodies to bury. I'll never worship the Sea again—no matter what the priests say!"

Pirra swallowed. "You sound as if it was my fault—"

"You're Yassassara's daughter," Sidayo said accusingly. "She dealt with the Crows—"

"That was before she found out what they're like," protested Pirra.

"She dealt with them!" insisted Sidayo. "That's why the Great Wave attacked Keftiu! That's why the Sun is gone and there will be no spring—because of her!"

Angry shouts from the crowd, and many shook their weapons at Pirra. She felt her blood rising in defense of her mother. Yassassara had been cold and harsh and she'd never loved any living creature—but she'd loved Keftiu, and she would have given her life for it. She did not deserve to be treated in such a way.

"How dare you speak of my mother like that," Pirra said between her teeth. "You have no idea—"

"And now you!" cut in Sidayo. "Coming here with that yellow-haired foreigner, bringing the Crows in your wake!"

More clenched fists and angry shouts.

"What's happening?" cried Hylas, who'd been getting increasingly restless. "What are they saying?"

"We thought we'd be safe in the mountains," Sidayo went on. "Safe from the Sea, safe from the Plague! But now you've brought the Crows. We saw them destroy Taka Zimi—and now you're leading them here, forcing us to hide in caves—"

"Pirra, what are they *saying*?" shouted Hylas.

"They blame my mother for everything," Pirra told him in Akean, "and they blame us because of the Crows."

"Listen to her talk to the stranger in his uncouth tongue!" shrilled Tanagra. "Who knows what they're plotting?"

Unable to contain himself, the man called Deukaryo leaped to his feet. "This must *stop*!" he bellowed.

The cavern fell silent.

In his ragged goatskins and battered felt cap, Deukaryo looked as if he was more accustomed to being part of the crowd than addressing it, but there was a strength about his burly figure that commanded attention.

"This girl," he told the others, "is the daughter of *Yassassara*. Yassassara, who gave Keftiu eighteen summers of peace and plenty! To treat her like this shames us all!"

A few people hung their heads, but Sidayo crossed his arms and snorted.

"Instead of insulting her," Deukaryo went on, "we should *help* her! Then maybe she can do what her mother could not—and bring back the Sun."

"Oh yes, look at her," sneered Sidayo. "I'll believe she can bring back the Sun when that stream outside turns to wine!"

That drew sniggers from the crowd, and Pirra flushed.

"Until then," Sidayo went on, "the Crows are still out there. So here's what we're going to do. We'll take the boy up the mountain and leave him to take his chances— and we'll keep the girl hostage. Then if we have to, we can give her to the Crows and they'll leave us in peace."

Shouts of approval. Deukaryo, overruled, shook his head in disgust.

"You can't do that," said Pirra in disbelief.

"What are they saying?" cried Hylas.

She told him in Akean, and he listened without expression. Then, still with his hands tied behind his back, he got to his feet. "Translate for me," he told her as he turned to face the crowd. With his fair hair and straight Lykonian nose, Pirra thought he looked utterly foreign; but his mouth was firm, and he had a rough authority that made everyone listen.

"Blaming Yassassara," he began, "gets you nowhere and misses the point."

Pirra hesitated, then repeated this in Keftian, provoking furious gasps—which Hylas ignored. "Skulking in caves won't get rid of the Crows," he went on, pausing now and then to let her translate. "Nor will giving them the girl. You can't *bargain* with the House of Koronos. Yassassara learned that before she died. There's a prophecy in my land. It says an Outsider will bring them down." He lifted his chin and squared his shoulders. "I am that Outsider. You Keftians call us the People of the Wild."

People stirred and exchanged uneasy glances, and Sidayo rubbed his thumb over his mouth. Deukaryo regarded Hylas thoughtfully from under his shaggy brows.

"I came to Mount Dikti," Hylas continued, "to find Yassassara's daughter. Now we must reach the House of the

Goddess. Together. We must get there before the Crows. If we don't, Keftiu is doomed." He scanned the weather-beaten faces, to let that sink in. "So. You have a choice. Either you help us, or you set us free and we do it on our own. But understand this." His eyes flicked to Pirra, and now she felt as if he spoke to her alone. "She and I stay together. We will not be separated again."

# 20

"I wonder if you persuaded them," Pirra said in a low voice.

Hylas glanced at her. "The one in the cap, what did he say to you?"

"He was defending us. And he seemed to think I . . ." She broke off with a frown.

"That you what?"

"Nothing." She didn't want to tell him what Deukaryo had said about bringing back the Sun.

They sat side by side with their backs against a rock, while their captors argued over their fate at the far end of the cavern.

A child came and set a waterskin before them. Pirra nodded her thanks, but the child only stared. She was a girl of about eight, in a ragged tunic much too big for her. Her face was pinched with hunger, and in one fist she clutched a grubby toy donkey of plaited straw. It flashed across Pirra's mind that if the Sun didn't return, this child and thousands like her would die.

A sturdy young man came and squatted beside them.

"My name is Teseo, son of Deukaryo," he told Hylas in heavily accented Akean. "You say you must reach the House of the Goddess before the Crows. Our leader says, then you go and we will see what you can do. Me and my father, my brother and sister, we take you out of the mountains as far as . . ." He glanced shyly at Pirra. "*Setoya*. I don't know it in Akean."

"The Mountain of the Earthshaker," she said.

Teseo nodded. "To *Setoya*. After that, you go alone."

———

"How come you speak Akean?" Hylas asked Teseo as they trudged through the snow, with Pirra and Deukaryo following behind.

"My mother," said Teseo. "She was slave from Akea. My father—he buy her freedom with his goats."

"I was a goatherd once," said Hylas.

Teseo blinked, and Hylas could see him wondering how a goatherd came to know the daughter of Yassassara.

Since dawn, Deukaryo had led them by secret passes and hidden trails, while his daughter Meta and his other son Lukuro scouted for Crows, ready to sound the alarm on rams' horns. To Hylas' relief he'd glimpsed Havoc keeping level with them through the trees. The others hadn't spotted her. She'd become much better at staying out of sight.

He was surprised to find himself trusting Deukaryo. Unlike Sidayo, Deukaryo was a herdsman who'd grown up on Mount Dikti, and he had a mountain man's habit of squinting at the sky to check the wind and weather. He treated Hylas with awkward respect as one of the People of the Wild, and seemed to regard Pirra with awe—especially after she held out her arm, and Echo swooped down and perched on her wrist.

As they descended into the foothills, they began to pass farmhouses marked with the white handprints of Plague. Deukaryo's heavy face grew anxious, and he gave everyone dittany to rub on their skin. Surreptitiously, Hylas also chewed a few of the buckthorn leaves Akastos had given him to ward off ghosts. In the mountains, he'd almost been able to forget them, but down here, he often got that ache in his temple, and felt their anger and loss shadowing his heart. He dreaded the haunted plain. And he knew that soon, he would have to tell Pirra.

That night, they camped under an overhang. Teseo woke up a fire, while Hylas cut pine boughs for bedding, and Pirra sat with her chin on her knees, looking spent.

After making an offering to the god of Mount Dikti, Deukaryo shared out gritty barley cakes and grayish olives, with a skinful of sour gray wine flavored with myrtle to mask the bitterness of ash. Then with a flourish he produced a small earthenware pot. "Honey," he said proudly. "The last we have."

Everyone dipped in their fingers and sucked the magical sweetness that came from the Sun and was gathered by bees. Hylas guessed that like him, they were thinking of long-ago days when the Sun still shone. Pensively, he broke off a chunk of honeycomb and crunched it. He realized that the others were staring at him.

"You eat *honeycomb*?" said Pirra.

"Why not?" he mumbled.

Rolling her eyes, she muttered something about Akeans in Keftian.

"I understood that," said Hylas—and everyone laughed.

After that, their guides relaxed. They tried to teach Hylas some Keftian, and smiled when he couldn't do the clicks.

"I do know one word," he said.

"Go on then," said Pirra, "let's hear it."

*"Rauko."*

She raised her eyebrows. "Not bad. Where'd you learn that?"

He told her about his encounter with the wild bull.

Deukaryo whistled. "You were lucky, my friend. Every spring the priests catch a wild bull and take it to *Kunisu*, for the bull-leapers to jump over. It takes years to learn, and someone's usually killed."

"Why do they do it?" said Hylas.

"To harness the power of the Earthshaker," said the herdsman, "and make the crops grow."

Hylas chewed an olive. "*Kunisu*, what's that?"

"The House of the Goddess," said Pirra. Her face contracted, and he guessed that she was dreading going back.

Deukaryo was watching her too. "Why do you need to reach Kunisu?" he said quietly.

Hylas and Pirra exchanged glances. "We have to find

something before the Crows get it," said Pirra.

To change the subject, Hylas said, "There's one other word you keep saying. *Pir-ákara?*"

The others grinned, and Pirra snorted a laugh. "That's me, you idiot! Pirra's short for Pirákara. It's my full name."

Hylas was taken aback. "You never told me that."

"Well, I don't tell you everything," she said.

He chewed another olive and spat out the stone. "I prefer Pirra."

"Good," she said. "So do I."

———

Pirra stumbled, and hoped the others hadn't noticed. She was exhausted, and her belly was knotted with tension. Every step took her closer to the House of the Goddess.

After three days' hard walking, they'd left the mountains and the snow behind, and crossed a cold, eerie plain of gray trees and Plague-marked villages, where the only moving things were drifting veils of windblown ash. Everyone was subdued, especially Hylas. At times he rubbed a small scar on his temple, and once he muttered that there were too many ghosts; but when she asked how he knew, he just shook his head.

On either side of them rose wooded ridges pocked with caves. Pirra didn't like the feel of them. They made her think of her mother in her tomb.

Beside her, Deukaryo cast her a thoughtful glance from under his heavy brows, and she knew that he still believed she could bring back the Sun.

"I can't do it," she told him in Keftian. "I'm not the High Priestess."

"You're her daughter," he said with simple faith.

"That's not enough to do a Mystery. It doesn't pass from mother to daughter; it's for the priests to choose the next High Priestess."

"I know," he said stubbornly, "but Yassassara had much power, and I think you do too. You have a bond with that bird, and falcons are creatures of the Goddess."

Pirra had no answer to that.

A little later, they saw the dark bulk of a mountain ahead, and the knot in her belly tightened.

"Setoya," Deukaryo said quietly.

Craning his neck, Hylas peered at the summit. "It looks like it's got horns."

"That's the shrine on top," said Pirra. "It has bulls' horns on the roof. That's why they call it the Mountain of the Earthshaker."

"They say it's always windy up there," said Deukaryo. "Noisy with the voices of the spirits. It's not far from Kunisu. The High Priestess used to go there to listen." He glanced at Pirra, but she turned away.

In the mountains, the snowglow had lightened the ashen twilight, but down here, the Great Cloud hung thicker than ever, and though it was mid-afternoon, it was so dark that bats mistook it for dusk and came pouring out of the caves like black smoke.

Echo sped after them—with predictably dismal results.

"Not bats, Echo," Pirra told her. "When will you learn to go after pigeons?" She tried to catch Hylas' eye, but he was anxiously scanning the caves on the ridge.

The real dusk came on, and they looked for somewhere to camp. Teseo spotted a likely cave, but Hylas insisted on checking it first. Pirra remembered that he'd done this before, and on impulse she followed him in.

Teseo had given her a rushlight, but its feeble glimmer only deepened the shadows, and she couldn't see Hylas.

The cave was dank, and smelled of dust and spiders. Broken pottery crunched beneath her boots, and to her alarm, she glimpsed small bronze offerings tucked into cracks.

"Hylas," she whispered. "We need to get out, this is a tomb!"

He didn't reply. As her eyes adjusted to the gloom, she saw him standing motionless with his back to her.

"Hylas—"

"Get away from me!" he whispered.

"It's me, Pirra!" But when she went to him his tawny eyes stared straight through her.

"Hylas?" She touched his hand. It felt clammy and cold. "Wake up."

He shuddered, rubbed his face, and seemed to see her for the first time. "This cave's no good," he mumbled, "Let's go."

The others accepted his judgment, and soon afterward they found another that he said was "clear," and made camp. Deukaryo went to confer with Lukuro and Meta, who would climb Setoya and keep watch for Crows, while Hylas busied himself helping Teseo waken a fire—as if, thought Pirra, he was avoiding her.

They ate a silent meal of gritty barley cakes, and when they'd finished, Deukaryo looked at Hylas and said calmly, "So tell me. How long have you been able to see ghosts?"

# 21

Hylas saw Pirra's eyes widen, and wished he'd had the courage to tell her before. "It started when I got to Keftiu," he told Deukaryo. "I—I can see Plague too. Like a black swarm. It's horrible. And I think it's getting worse. How did you know?"

"I didn't," the herdsman said simply. "I guessed. The ghosts . . . do you see them all the time?"

Hylas shook his head. "Only now and then. I never know when it's going to happen, but I get an ache." He touched his temple.

"You have a scar," said Pirra in a low voice.

He glanced at her, but she wouldn't meet his eyes. "It was a burn," he said. As he described his ordeal in the fiery mountain of Thalakrea, he seemed once again to smell the sulfurous smoke; he saw the burning shadow of the Lady of Fire, and Her bright hair blazing in the black air; he felt the searing touch of Her finger on his temple . . . "D'you think that's why?" he cried. "Because the Lady burned me?"

"Don't you?" said Deukaryo.

"I—never thought of it. What does it mean?"

Deukaryo watched the sparks shooting upward. "I'm no seer," he said, "but I know that everyone has a door in their minds between this world and that of the spirits. In most of us this door is hidden by a veil until we die. With you, I think maybe the Lady scorched that veil away. At least in part. Maybe that's why you only sometimes see ghosts: because the shreds of the veil blow back and forth across your sight."

"Whatever it is, I hate it," muttered Hylas.

Deukaryo's mouth twisted. "Ah, the gods don't care about that, my friend. And it helped us tonight, didn't it? So maybe it brings good as well as bad."

"Now you're talking like a seer," said Hylas.

Deukaryo chuckled and clapped him on the shoulder. "Then it's time we got some sleep!"

---

Later, Pirra woke to find Deukaryo and Teseo snoring, but Hylas gone.

Quietly, she stepped around the sleepers and left the cave. It wasn't as cold as in the mountains, but the night was sharp, and she pulled her dirty fox furs about her. The fire at the mouth of the cave had burned low, but the embers gave off a faint red glow. "Hylas?" she called softly.

No answer.

"Echo? Echo, I need you . . ."

Echo glided down and alighted on her shoulder. Pirra

fumbled at her belt for the vole that Teseo had caught earlier, and the falcon ripped it hungrily to shreds.

Sadly, Pirra stroked Echo's scaly foot. Often when she was with the falcon, she thought of Userref. She was worried about him. Deukaryo had heard no word of any wandering Egyptian, so where was he? She pictured him freezing on Mount Dikti, or captured by the Crows.

Hylas loomed out of the dark, saw her, and stopped. "I went to find Havoc," he said.

"And did you?"

"She found me. I *think* she understands that we can't be together for a bit, but I wish I was sure." With his heel he hacked at the ground. "Pirra, I was going to tell you. About the—about what I can see."

"Doesn't matter," she replied.

Squatting on his heels, he dug at the earth with a stick.

"When it happens," she said, "do you get scared?"

"Yes," he said without raising his head. "It wasn't so bad in the mountains, but down here there are so many. They're lost and *angry*, and I can't help. And it's getting stronger."

Pirra's chest tightened. There might be ghosts in the House of the Goddess. And watching over it from her tomb, there would be Yassassara, sitting up in her coffin.

Hylas was looking at her. "You're afraid of going back," he said quietly.

She nodded.

"But it's empty, isn't it? There'll be nobody to stop you leaving."

She hesitated. "There aren't any people there, if that's what you mean."

Echo finished the vole and wiped her beak on Pirra's furs, then flew off, disappearing silently into the night.

"We'll be together the whole time," said Hylas, "and then we'll leave."

Pirra didn't reply.

Again he stabbed the ground. "Is something else worrying you?"

"Why do you ask?"

"There's a look you get when Deukaryo talks to you in Keftian. You had it now. Is it about your mother?"

She stared at him. "Sometimes, Hylas, I wish you didn't notice *everything*."

His lip curled. "Well, I do, so why don't you just tell me?"

Again she hesitated. "That rite I told you about—the Mystery she was going to do before she died. Deukaryo thinks I should do it in her place."

"And—can you?"

"Of course not! This isn't merely some sacrifice. She was the *High Priestess*, and not even she knew if it would work! She'd have been the first to say I couldn't do it."

Throwing away the stick, he rose to his feet. "Well, like I said, we won't be in there long. We'll go in fast, get the dagger, and get out."

He made it sound so simple. But he'd never even been

to the House of the Goddess, he didn't know what it was like. And he had no idea what performing the Mystery would mean. If he knew, he'd be appalled that she was even considering it.

Because what if Deukaryo was right, and she *could* do it? The thought made Pirra turn cold.

I can't, she told herself. I'm not brave enough. Not for that.

---

Hylas was jolted awake by the booming of rams' horns. The scouts on Setoya were sounding a warning, and Deukaryo was leaning over him.

"Crows," hissed the herdsman, "on the other side of that ridge, we've got to get moving!"

Hurriedly, they buried the embers and set off into the dark. Hylas felt sick with fatigue. Beside him, Pirra was grimly silent.

Pebbles rattled onto the trail, and two shadowy figures skittered down the slope in front of them. Lukuro whispered to his father in Keftian, then Meta broke in and Pirra protested.

Deukaryo cut them short and turned to Hylas. "Can you see that gorge up ahead? Follow it, keep to the river, it'll take you to Kunisu."

"How far?" said Hylas.

"Half a day or so if you hurry."

"What about you?" said Pirra.

"We'll decoy them up Setoya and lose them on the

other side. You and Meta swap cloaks. With luck they'll think she's you."

"That's too dangerous!" whispered Pirra. "She might get shot!"

"We know this mountain, they don't," said Deukaryo. "Hurry! It's the only way!"

# 22

"The prisoner says this is the way to the top," said Ilarkos.

"It leads to the shrine, yes?" panted Kreon.

Ilarkos translated that into Keftian, and the captive gave a terrified nod.

"Then let's go." Kreon tore off his wolf-fur mantle and flung it to a slave.

Telamon hesitated. It wasn't yet dawn, and the Mountain of the Earthshaker loomed black against the charcoal sky. The men's torches were feeble glimmers in the dark, and from time to time he heard the echoing boom of rams' horns. Who knew what awaited them up there?

"I said let's go!" barked Kreon.

As they climbed higher, the wind whirled ash in Telamon's face and whipped his cloak about his legs. Something felt wrong. If Hylas and Pirra were heading for the shrine, why were they blowing horns?

Below, he made out the dim line of the river snaking north to the House of the Goddess. A startling idea came to him, and he ran to catch up with Kreon. "This doesn't feel right," he said in a low voice, so that the men wouldn't hear.

"Nothing about this cursed country feels right," snarled his uncle.

"I mean, what if it's a trick?"

"What?" snapped Kreon.

"What if they're not here, on the mountain?"

"And what if they're up at that shrine right now, calling on the gods to destroy our dagger? Do *you* want to tell Koronos that they succeeded and we *failed*?"

Telamon swallowed. "But if you're wrong—"

"You saw the girl as well as I did!"

"I saw *a* girl at a distance, in the dark! I'm not even sure it was her!"

"And if it was?"

Telamon bit his lip. "Why don't we split up? You take half the men to the top, I'll take the others to the House of the Goddess—"

"What will you do when you get there?" sneered Kreon. "What if it's not empty? They say it's as big as a mountain! Could you conquer it with twenty men? You're not even a warrior!"

Telamon flushed. "If I'm right, and I get the dagger—"

"Oh, so that's your game," cut in Kreon. "You want to be the one to put it in Koronos' hands; you'd turn him against me, wouldn't you? Well maybe, just to be sure, we should split up. Maybe we'll send half the men up the mountain, with Ilarkos to lead them—and *I'll* take the rest to the House of the Goddess!"

Telamon opened his mouth to reply—but at that moment, dawn broke and in the distance, a shaft of ashen light revealed a strange, glimmering hill.

Kreon sucked in his breath with a hiss. Their Keftian captive sank to his knees and murmured, "*Kunisu*."

"H-he says it's the House of the Goddess," faltered Ilarkos.

For a heartbeat, as Telamon beheld the ancient heart of Keftian power, he was overwhelmed. Then he remembered Hylas and Pirra taunting him at the edge of the gorge, and his spirit hardened. He pictured himself leading a daring raid to seize the House of the Goddess. He would brandish the dagger of Koronos and proclaim himself ruler of all Keftiu—and Hylas would be dead, and Pirra would kneel before him in homage . . .

Kreon's harsh voice wrenched him back. "Nephew! Did you hear what I said?"

"She's not here," said Telamon. "Send Ilarkos up to the shrine if you like, but it's a trick. They're taking it to the House of the Goddess."

How much farther? Hylas wondered uneasily.

Pirra ran beside him with her fists clenched, and Havoc trotted behind. She'd joined them soon after they'd fled the camp, appearing silently, as lions do, and seeming to sense that this was no time for lengthy greetings.

At first they'd stumbled along the river in the dark, not daring to use the rushlights Deukaryo had given them. As dawn broke, they'd made out hills dotted with farms, and olive groves, vineyards, barley fields: all abandoned and gray with ash. It was now around noon, and Setoya was far behind. They'd heard no sounds of pursuit. Had Deukaryo's trick worked?

It grew warmer. Flies buzzed and sparrows chirped in the Sunless gloom. Hylas took off his jerkin and tied it around his waist. To his right, a shadowy ridge frowned down on them, pitted with caves. He didn't like the feel of it.

Havoc wrinkled her nose in the odd half-snarl that meant she'd caught a strong scent.

"She can smell the town," said Pirra in a taut voice.

"There's a *town*?" said Hylas.

"It surrounds Kunisu on three sides, with the river to the east. But it'll be deserted. Come on. Not far now."

Hylas peered at the ridge. "If the Crows get up there, they'll pick us off as easy as spearing fish in a barrel."

"They wouldn't dare go up there," said Pirra in a strange voice.

"Why not?"

She didn't reply.

Havoc was also gazing at the ridge, her eyes following things Hylas couldn't see. With a jolt, he realized that the caves were sealed with rocks. Pain stabbed his temple, and from the tail of his eye, he glimpsed black swarms of Plague, and shadowy figures emanating rage and loss. "They're tombs," he hissed. "Hundreds of them!"

"Yes," said Pirra. "And more in the hills to the west and north. They're all around Kunisu. The cities of the Dead."

He shot her a glance. "Your mother—is she—"

"Yes. They buried her high on the Ridge of the Dead. She's looking down on us."

Before he could speak, she was hurrying ahead. Then the trees before them thinned and they emerged into the open—and Hylas gasped.

Before him sprawled a vast jumble of ash-gray houses, packed together like some impossibly huge village around a pale glimmering hill. But it *wasn't* a hill; it was a stronghold bigger and more astonishing than any he could have imagined. Its walls were eerily smooth and untouched by ash, their tops spiked with giant stone horns of bulls. Even in this Sunless half-light, it possessed an unearthly radiance, as if lit from within.

"Kunisu," said Pirra with an odd mix of bitterness and pride. "The House of the Goddess."

———

At that moment, horns boomed in the distance, and Havoc took fright and fled for the woods.

"Havoc, come back!" cried Hylas. But the lion cub was gone.

Pirra grabbed his wrist. "Come on, it's not far now!"

"But Havoc—she'll never follow us through a town!"

"No time to go and find her! Come *on*, let's get this over with!"

She was right. With a last desperate glance over his shoulder, Hylas followed her into the bewildering warren that was the town.

He had a blurred impression of towering walls and dark doorways, many with pus-eaters squatting outside. Then they were racing up a trail of treacherously smooth blue stone. On either side rose walls of green stone cut in blocks so huge, they must have been hewn by gods. Gates loomed ahead, encrusted with gilded Sea creatures—octopuses, flying fish, dolphins—and flanked by man-high wax figures speckled with Plague.

The giant gates looked shut, but when Pirra pushed, they creaked open, exhaling a whiff of incense and sulfur.

Pirra took his hand. Her fingers were icy, her face pale and set. "Stay close," she said. "Strangers get lost inside."

In his whole life, Hylas had only ever been in peasants' huts, and once, Kreon's stronghold. Nothing like this.

He was running along a dim passage painted with dizzying blue spirals. The floor was unnaturally smooth and patterned with swirling red and yellow waves. The slatted roof let in bars of gray daylight, so that Pirra flickered in and out of sight.

"We'll need the rushlights," she muttered.

Hylas lit two with his strike-fire, and around him a magic land sprang to life. Black swallows swooped in a blood-red sky over waving blue reeds and ice-white lilies. A green lion spread its yellow wings and uttered a silent roar.

"They're paintings, Hylas," said Pirra. "Follow me. I hid the dagger in my room, it's on the other side. And mind your step."

Glancing warily about her, she led him along twisting passages, across ditches that she called drains, past dead ends and sudden alarming drops. More painted worlds flashed past. Hylas felt very much an intruder: a rough Akean goatherd, far out of his depth.

Nothing here was as it seemed. The wall beneath his hand was cool white stone polished to shell-like smoothness, but a few paces on, it became a wooden screen that rocked at his touch. Some doors were wide enough for three to walk abreast. Others were narrow and flanked by tall red pillars with broad shoulders, like men standing guard. Hylas edged past, taking care not to touch.

Pirra ran straight into another door that turned out to be a curtain of crystal droplets that parted like frozen rain. He blundered into a hanging of slippery purple stuff that clung to his face like cobwebs; Pirra said it was silk, and made by worms. In a dim windowless chamber, he glimpsed baskets with snakes coiled at the bottom, fast asleep. "For rites," muttered Pirra. "Later I'll check if they need food."

Now they were crossing an echoing hall where it felt as if people had only just left. Hylas barked his shins on a gilded bench with feet like claws, and nearly overturned a table set with clay drinking cups finer than eggshell. He could see no hearth, and he asked how they kept warm.

"We don't have hearths," murmured Pirra, "we use braziers."

So even the fires move about, he thought in alarm.

Now she was heading up a series of stepping stones, very flat and straight. "Careful on the stairs," she warned.

Is that what they are, thought Hylas.

"And keep close to the inside wall." On the outer edge, there *was* no wall, just a lethal drop.

They turned into a passage with doors on either side; the doors were tied shut by cords that had been sealed with clay. "The storerooms," said Pirra. "Once we've got the dagger, we'll come back for food."

Wherever they went, Hylas sensed no ghosts—but he caught the furtive noises of many unseen creatures. Sparrows and martins fluttered overhead, and he glimpsed a wasps' nest on a roofbeam, and a snake's tail flickering down a drain. Once, he heard a distant scrape of hooves. It seemed that after the people moved out, the wild had moved in.

He worried about Havoc. She would never dare follow him in here, and she wouldn't understand why he'd gone. She would think he'd abandoned her all over again.

More passages, more rooms. "Workshops," said Pirra.

"Who works in them?"

"Oh, weavers, potters, seal-cutters, gold-workers . . ."

"How do you find your way in all this?"

She gave him a grim smile. "I've spent my whole life in here. I've had nothing to do but find my way."

Strange images leaped out at him from the workshops. A ceiling furred with a colony of sleeping bats, like lumpy black fruit. A pile of giant eggs, each bigger than a child's head, and a stack of what appeared to be enormous tusks, taller than a man.

"The eggs are from a bird," said Pirra, "I think it's called ostrich. The tusks are ivory, from Egypt, some kind of monster. There's an ivory god with golden hair in the Hall of Whispers . . ."

*Whispers, whispers,* echoed the walls.

"We'll take a shortcut across the Great Court," she said, pushing open a door and leading him out into daylight.

He found himself in a vast open space floored in yellow with a dizzying pattern of blue ivy leaves. The walls all around were two stories high, with gilded doors and tall windows, more red guardian columns, and a vast painted crowd, watching him.

Everywhere he turned, he saw haughty men and pale women of staggering beauty, with dark almond-shaped eyes that reminded him of Pirra's. They looked so real that he felt they were only waiting for him to leave, so that they could start talking about him. *What's that Outsider doing here?*

At the heart of the Great Court stood an olive tree in a huge gilded pot—and at the north end, a giant double axe of gleaming bronze, mounted on a pedestal of purple stone before a yawning darkness.

"That's the ramp leading down to the understory," said Pirra.

"You mean—there's *more,* underneath?"

Again that mirthless smile. "Oh, yes. Above us too."

She pointed to a ledge high on the west wall. "That's the balcony where my mother stands. I mean—stood."

Hylas licked his lips. "What do they do out here?"

"Bull-leaping. Dancing. Sacrifices. Sometimes, when my mother was away, Userref used to give me rides in the chariot . . ." She frowned. "Come on. Nearly there."

Another passage, this one painted with deer as big as real ones. Hylas glimpsed a buck about to twitch a fly off its ear, and a dormouse on a barley spike, its painted tail curled around the stem.

Pirra had disappeared round a corner. He ran to catch up—and came face-to-face with a bull.

"Pirra, watch out!" he yelled, whipping out his axe.

"It's all right, it's not real!"

The wild bull was even bigger than the one he'd encountered in the foothills, and it was charging with its head down. Hylas took in its bulging shoulder muscles and thick lolling tongue. Some god had turned it to stone as it half emerged from the wall.

"*Looks* real," he muttered, ashamed at being fooled.

"When I was little," said Pirra, "I used to think it came alive at night."

Maybe it does, thought Hylas as he edged past, trying not to catch the bull's bloodshot red eye.

They reached a dim windowless chamber guarded by more broad-shouldered columns. Hylas' rushlight revealed painted fishes on the walls, a splendid claw-footed bench of gilded wood, a scarlet rug sewn with blue swallows, a tall lamp of purple marble, and a cedarwood chest inlaid with ivory panels.

He swallowed. "Is this where the Goddess lives?"

Pirra snorted. "Course not, it's just my room."

Her *room*? He was aghast. He'd always known she was rich. He'd never pictured this.

"The dagger's over there behind a wall panel," muttered Pirra. "Hold my light while I—" She broke off.

"What is it?" said Hylas.

In the gloom, he made out a hole low down in the wall, and a thin square of glittery white stone beside it on the floor. Near that lay a staff and a goatskin that had been flung aside in a rush.

"It's gone," Pirra said blankly. "The dagger's gone."

## 23

"Userref took it," said Pirra. "That means he's alive, thank the Goddess!"

"You're sure it was him?" said Hylas.

"Has to be, he's the only one who knows where I hid it. Look, there's the proof. I wrapped it in that goatskin, but Egyptians think goats are unclean, so he used the staff to get at the dagger without touching the hide. Oh, Userref." She sat on the bed, feeling numb. "I should've known he'd come straight here. And he knew the way, that's why he got here first."

"So he really does think you're dead," said Hylas. "Where will he have gone?"

She shook her head. "I told him to keep it safe till he could destroy it. He may still be in here, hiding out."

"He can't be, we've been all over."

"Hylas, we've hardly been anywhere! Kunisu's vast. He could be in any one of the workshops or the inner chambers or down in the understory—"

"And if Deukaryo's trick didn't work and the Crows are

on our trail, they'll be coming after us right now and we won't know it, stuck in here."

She met his eyes. "There are places we can see out."

"Right. And while we're checking, we can look for Userref."

Time passed in a blur as they raced between windows and balconies. As they ran, Pirra tried to give Hylas a sense of Kunisu. "Great Court's in the middle. My chambers are to the east, with my mother's above. Workshops in the west. Storerooms to the north, with the understory underneath . . ." But she could see that he was struggling to take it in.

Wherever they went, they saw no sign of the Crows— or of Userref. Once, Hylas opened his mouth to call his name, but was instantly hushed by Pirra. "We don't know what the priests left in here to guard it," she whispered. "Best not make too much noise."

Hylas licked his lips. "Dark soon. I say we hide out in your room and continue the search at first light."

He was right, but Pirra felt a stab of alarm. They'd planned to find the dagger and get out—but Kunisu wasn't letting them go.

Hylas asked if there were other entrances apart from the gates, and when she said yes, he was horrified. "What if they're open too?"

To their relief, they found the north and south gates securely barred. Then they doubled back and barred the west gates, which they hadn't done when they'd come in.

"I wonder why they were open in the first place," said Hylas, voicing Pirra's thoughts.

"Must have been Userref," she said. But it occurred to her that maybe Userref had also found the gates ajar. Maybe Yassassara had ordered them left like that—because she'd foreseen that her daughter would return.

It was dark by the time they made their final check at the East Balcony. Below them the ground fell away to trees and the river. No glimmer of torches. No sign of the Crows.

"Which doesn't mean they're not out there," muttered Hylas.

Pirra didn't reply. To the southeast and horribly close, she made out the Ridge of the Dead. There was no mistaking her mother's tomb. It was sealed with white gypsum and it glared down at her like a great cold eye.

". . . if we don't find him tomorrow," Hylas was saying, "we get out. Pirra?"

"What? Um. Yes."

But as they headed back to her room, she had the dreadful feeling that things were unfolding exactly as her mother had wanted.

She was back in the House of the Goddess, and she was never getting out.

---

The lion cub couldn't see any way of getting in.

The boy and girl had raced into the gaping jaws of the great horned mountain, but the cub's courage had failed her and she'd fled. Now she crouched among reeds by the fast-flowing wet, shaking with terror.

She'd never seen a mountain like this. It was white and smooth and hollow, and it reeked of men. Around it were many lairs of men, all empty, but still with that terrifying reek. She couldn't go in there, not even for the boy.

The Dark came and the cub smelled prey making their way to drink. A doe trotted past without sensing her, and a badger shambled out of its hole within an easy pounce. The lion cub ignored them. The falcon swept past with a scornful glance, and the lion cub ignored her too. The boy might be in trouble. *He might never come out.*

Leaving the reeds, she prowled closer, and gazed up at the horned mountain. She still couldn't face its gaping jaws, but maybe she could find a less frightening way in.

The mountain's flanks were hard, and so smooth that her claws didn't make a scratch—she just slid off, leaving a smear of dusty paw prints.

She spotted a pine growing near it. One branch reached even closer. The branch was quite high up, but from there it would be an easy leap inside . . .

Pines have good rough bark, and the lion cub managed her best climb ever and scrambled into a fork and considered what to do next.

The branch she was aiming for was on the other side of the trunk. Awkwardly, she stretched one forepaw around and caught it with her claws. She made a swipe with the other forepaw—missed, hung by one paw, scrabbling frantically—then swung up a hind leg and hoisted herself clumsily onto the branch, where she crouched, clinging with every claw and even her tail.

The falcon lit onto the same branch and stared at her.

The cub hissed at her to get *off*, and the falcon flew away and perched on one of the mountain's horns, to watch.

The branch was higher than the lion cub had thought, and much farther from the mountain than it had looked from the ground. She could never leap that far.

The falcon lifted off and lazily circled the pine, then glided between the mountain's tall white horns and disappeared inside. *See? It's easy for me.*

Oh, go away. The cub tried to turn around, but the branch was too narrow. To reach the fork and get down again, she'd have to go backward—but she'd never done that before, not this high up.

Now that the falcon was gone, the cub wished she'd return. The bird was haughty and infuriating, but she was better than being on your own.

A gust of wind ruffled the cub's fur, and the pine tree whispered: *What are you going to do now?*

# 24

Just for tonight, Pirra told herself stubbornly, I'm going to forget about the Mystery. I'm fed up with being dirty and scared.

Making Hylas wait in her chamber, she ran next door to the water room and took a swift cold bath, then dragged a comb through her hair and threw on the clean tunic she'd brought from her clothes chest. After that she hurriedly showed Hylas the split seat in the corner for relieving oneself, with the bucket to wash it away, and then explained about refilling the bath from the water jars and pulling out the wooden plug when he'd finished.

He eyed the bath with suspicion. "That's a coffin."

"No it's not."

"Yes it is. Last time I saw one of them was in a tomb."

"It's a *bath*," said Pirra, "and you could do with one. I'll be back soon, I'm off to get supplies."

She found the cloth stores locked, and cracked the clay sealings with her knife, half expecting an angry steward to come running. Her rushlight revealed piles of linen and wool that exhaled a dusty tang of rosemary. Stifling a sense of wrong-doing, she found a short-sleeved jerkin of fine blue wool that looked about Hylas' size, a man's kilt of supple deerskin with a fringed hem, a wide red calf-hide belt, sandals, and a knife-sheath of braided leather. Bundling them up in a cloak of rare dark green, she made for the food stores.

Someone had broken in before her: someone who hated stealing, and had left a neat record of what they'd taken on a waxed wooden tablet propped against the door—four flatbreads, a wineskin, and a bag of salted ducks' legs.

In the wax, Pirra saw the tiny imprint of a scarab beetle. The reluctant thief had been Userref. "Userref?" she whispered.

No answer.

Her hand went to the *wedjat* amulet at her throat. She longed for Userref to emerge from the shadows and scold her. "Pirra, look at you! Hair loose—and your *feet*! Rougher than a crocodile's hide!"

"Userref, where *are* you?" she said in a hoarse whisper. But all she heard was the thrum of sparrows' wings, and mice scurrying along the roof beams.

She knew the priests wouldn't have left Kunisu unprotected. There would be guardians—although maybe not in human form. Suddenly she was sharply aware of the dark spaces around her. The glimmering rushlight made familiar things frightening. A painted octopus glared from a grain jar as tall as a man.

Her thoughts flew to Echo. Did the falcon know where

she was? Would she dare follow her into Kunisu?

"Food," she told herself firmly. "Get on with it, Pirra."

Hurrying down the rows, she grabbed as much as she could carry, then struggled back to her quarters as laden as a donkey on market day.

Hylas was still in the water room, splashing in the bath. She flung in his new clothes, then started setting out the supplies on her clothes chest.

"Did you find him?" he called.

"No. But he was here." Standing back, she surveyed the feast. There were snails in oil and octopus in brine; smoked venison, dried swordfish, and blood sausage with onions and chestnuts; pickled vine leaves stuffed with fennel and chickpeas; pressed figs, fat black mulberries in rose-petal syrup; and her favorite, crunchy almond honey cakes. To drink, she'd brought a skin of best raisin wine, with barley meal and ewe's-milk cheese for mixing, and two silver drinking cups, because they were lighter than pottery and wouldn't break.

While she was away, Hylas had found some pressed olive kernels and woken a fire in the brazier, so as she waited for him she made an offering, flicking wine on the flames and begging the Goddess to keep away the Crows.

Please, she added silently, tell me if I should do the Mystery. Send me a sign. Is this why You're keeping me here? Or is it just chance?

She must have spoken the last bit out loud, because behind her Hylas said, "Is what just chance?"

He stood in the doorway wearing his new jerkin and kilt, and for a moment he didn't look like Hylas, but the long-legged god in the Hall of Whispers: the same broad shoulders and narrow waist; the same knife-cut features and startling rock-crystal eyes.

"Is what just chance?" he repeated.

"Nothing," she croaked. "I was making an offering."

He nodded. "Did the gods send you a sign?"

"Not yet."

He glanced at the food on the chest, then back to her. "You look better."

She touched her cheek. She'd never felt so ugly, or hated her scar more. "I'm just clean, that's all," she muttered.

He tucked his lion-claw amulet in the neck of his jerkin and raised his eyebrows. "Do I look Keftian?"

She flushed. "No. But you look all right."

---

Pirra lit more lamps and fetched some sheepskins, then they sat on the floor and fell on the food. She gulped two goblets of wine very fast, and felt her worries slip away in a golden glow. She forgot about the Mystery. She even forgot about her scar. It was wonderful to be warm again, and *clean*.

Hazily, she watched Hylas feeding the fire. The light caught a dusting of fine gold hairs along his jaw. No Keftian man wore a beard, and Pirra had always thought them uncouth, but she reflected that if Hylas grew one, she wouldn't mind.

He'd resumed his place on the floor and sat turning his drinking cup in his fingers and staring at the paintings on the wall. He hadn't drunk as much as her, and to her surprise, he seemed ill at ease in his new clothes. He'd ignored the sandals, and kept his battered old knife-sheath. She wondered why.

"Why do they do that?" he said abruptly.

"What?"

"Keftian children, like the one in that painting. Shave their heads, with one lock hanging down."

"To keep cool. And it's cleaner. But you always leave the sidelock because that's where your soul lives."

He stared at her. "*You* did it too?"

"Till I was eleven." She smiled. He didn't smile back.

It occurred to her that maybe he felt intimidated by Kunisu, so to put him at his ease, she asked what he thought of the dolphins on the other wall, and if they reminded him of Spirit, the dolphin they'd made friends with two summers ago.

"They got the noses wrong," he said. "They look like ducks."

"I think so too," she agreed. "And the fins are wrong. Spirit wouldn't think much of them, would he?"

He gave her a brief smile, but it soon clouded over.

"Hylas, what's wrong?" she said.

"Nothing."

"That's not true."

He hesitated. "I just . . . I never thought it would be

this grand. I mean, your own little coffin, just to wash!"

"It's a bath," she said, biting back a smile.

"And all the colored clothes and jewels and silver cups—*silver!*"

"And no earth, no trees, and no freedom," she said bitterly.

He glowered at her, unconvinced.

"The first time I ever saw a live fish," she said, "I was astonished because it moved so fast. I'd only seen them in paintings or a dish." She paused. "There was an old woman, a slave who'd never been outside, she'd worked in the weaving room her whole life. One day she found her way to the Great Court and saw the sky. She was terrified it would fall on her; it sent her mad. I've always dreaded ending up like her. Gibbering in some windowless room with only lizards for company."

Hylas gave her a considering look. "That's not going to happen. If we don't find Userref first thing tomorrow, we're getting out."

She nodded. She wanted to believe it. She really did.

"Pirra, what's wrong?" said Hylas. "Are you still worrying about the Mystery? Is it—dangerous?"

Springing to her feet, Pirra grabbed the oil jar and fed the lamps. Sometimes, Hylas noticed too much.

"Whatever it involves," he said quietly, "I'll help you."

"You can't. You can't help and I can't tell you about it."

"Why?"

"Because . . . it's secret. That's why it's a Mystery. All I can tell you is it's about calling on the Goddess to make Herself visible—to make Herself flesh—then *maybe*, She'll bring back the Sun." She gulped more wine, but it no longer gave her a warm glow, only a sick feeling in the pit of her stomach.

She felt the weight of expectation tightening around her. Her mother . . . Deukaryo . . . that child in the cavern with her grubby toy donkey, and all the others like her . . .

She couldn't tell Hylas any of this. He would only try to stop her. And if she did find the courage to perform the Mystery, it would mean never seeing him again.

It would mean sacrificing her life to bring back the Sun.

# 25

The falcon was worried that she might never find the girl. She *missed* her. And she could feel that the girl was in trouble.

The mountain was a strange echoing place with many narrow tunnels and lines of weirdly straight tree trunks with neither branches nor leaves. The falcon liked all the colors, and as she searched for the girl, she had fun practicing her flying by racing in and out between the tree trunks.

Now she was speeding through an echoey cave full of the musky smell of earthbound beasts. She glimpsed something huge moving in the dark. Then she was out again and there was another line of tree trunks, so she did some more in-and-out flying.

She nearly crashed into a giant shimmery cobweb— swerved, and bashed her wingtip against something hard that rattled alarmingly.

Frightened, the falcon perched on a ledge. She didn't like this place anymore. There was no earth and no Wind, and that giant cobweb had nearly gotten her.

To her surprise, she found herself missing the lion cub. The cub was grumpy and had an irritating habit of sneaking up when you were trying to roost, but you always knew what she was feeling. The falcon found that oddly comforting.

Bobbing her head to sharpen her sight, she set off again. More narrow tunnels, more leafless tree trunks; but this time, she did no in-and-out flying. Sparrows scattered before her and lizards darted into cracks. Although she was hungry, the falcon ignored them all.

Where was the girl?

It was getting late.

Pirra sat on her bed, gazing at the fire. Hylas thought she must be thinking about the Mystery, and all the other things that daughters of High Priestesses think about, which Lykonian goatherds can't possibly understand.

She was flushed from the wine, and looked handsomer than he'd ever seen her. Her hair was a shadowy river down her back, and her dark eyes reminded him of the painted women in the Great Court: just as highborn and just as inaccessible.

It was a long time since he'd thought about the difference between them, but now it became a chasm.

She'd dressed in a rush, which made it worse, because she was so used to it all. Her tunic was fine scarlet wool patterned with blue lilies made of tiny glittering stones that she called beads. At her waist, with casual grace, she'd knotted a belt of gold lizard skin with two silver tassels hanging down. When she moved, he caught a heady scent of jasmine.

What an idiot he'd been. He'd actually imagined that she could live with him and Issi and Havoc on Mount Lykas. Idiot. You can't take a girl like this to live on a mountain.

"D'you want more wine?" she said suddenly.

"No," he replied.

She gave him a look that he didn't understand. Then she rose and spread the red rug carefully over her bed, and looked at him again.

She's trying to put me at my ease, he thought savagely. Because I'm an ex-slave with scars on my knees from crawling down mines, and part of my earlobe cut off to remove the mark of the Outsider.

He got to his feet, overturning his cup with a clatter. "We should get some sleep," he growled.

"Right," said Pirra.

"I'll sleep in the passage."

She touched her scar. "Right," she said again. "But you don't need to. I mean"—her flush deepened—"there's a bed in the next room."

He snorted. "I've never slept in a bed in my life and I'm not going to now."

She drew a breath. "I'll fetch you more sheepskins."

He'd never slept in those either, but he wasn't going to tell her, so he watched her bring an armful of the cleanest fleeces he'd ever seen, along with a small soft pad. "What's that?" he said.

"It's a pillow. It's—for your head."

"Oh." Yet another thing he'd never heard of.

"Sleep well," she mumbled. Her eyes were glittering, as if she was going to cry, and suddenly he wondered if he'd got it all wrong. He made to speak, but she let down the door-hanging between them.

"You too," he muttered.

Silence on the other side. He pictured her standing there. Then he heard the whisper of her bare feet crossing the floor and the creak of her bed.

Still with the nagging sense that he'd made a mistake, he kicked the sheepskins along the passage. They were incredibly soft and smelled faintly of jasmine; curling up in them was like having his own little cloud. He'd scarcely closed his eyes when sleep reached up and dragged him under.

He dreamed he was standing beneath the Mountain of the Earthshaker, craning his neck at the peak. It turned into a huge bull and came thundering after him. Now he was in the House of the Goddess, running down endless passages, trying to find Pirra. He ran out into the Great Court and there she was, but to his horror, she'd become one of the painted women on the walls, and she was laughing at him. *What are you doing here, Outsider?*

He woke with a start. He was hot and tangled in sheepskins. He could still hear Pirra's mocking laughter from the dream.

He hated Kunisu. He hated feeling these unnaturally smooth stones beneath him instead of earth, and these painted walls that shut him off from wind and sky.

He sat up. It was no good, he was never going to sleep.

Pirra lay curled in her scarlet rug, her face buried in her pillow in a storm of dark hair. She didn't stir when he lit a rushlight from the brazier. He would climb to that place where you could see out—the East Balcony?—and make sure there were still no Crows. At least that was something he could do.

By night, the House of the Goddess was alive with the secret rustlings of wild creatures. He found the stairs easily enough, and left his rushlight in an empty brazier before stepping onto the balcony. If anyone was out there, he didn't want them seeing his light.

To his relief, the woods along the river were dark: no red sparks of torches or campfires. He caught the tang of pine, and made out a tree not far from where he stood. He wished he was out in the forest.

The stairs seemed longer on the way back, and he heard a mysterious rhythmic clicking, some way off. At the bottom, he blundered into a silk hanging. That hadn't been there on the way out, he must've taken a wrong turn. In the mountains, he hardly ever got lost, but in here, everything looked the same.

That clicking was louder. He came to a shadowy hall where a massive loom leaned against the wall. Along its lower edge hung a row of clay weights, clicking against each other.

His scalp tightened. There was no draft that could've set them moving. Who—or what—had passed this way?

He swung his rushlight to and fro—and a painted face glared at him from the wall.

The Goddess wore a skirt of overlapping blue waves and a tight red open-breasted bodice. Her white features and fierce dark stare reminded him of Pirra's mother, the High Priestess.

He thought of the ghosts on the Ridge of the Dead. Did they come down by night and walk the silent halls of Kunisu?

Was Yassassara here now?

He ran.

More stairs, more passages. He burst through a doorway into the Great Court. Wherever he turned, painted crowds mocked him silently. *Which way, Outsider?*

He chose a door at random and was relieved to recognize the paintings in the passage. There was that buck with the fly on its ear, and the dormouse on the barley spike; a few more paces and he'd reach the stone bull half emerging from the wall—

The bull was gone.

In disbelief, Hylas passed his hands over the smooth cold stone where it had been. This was the place, he was sure of it.

With a prickle of fear, he remembered Pirra telling him how when she was little, she used to believe that it came alive at night . . .

In the passage ahead, he heard the scrape of hooves, and loud snorting animal breath.

His rushlight shrank to a dim glow.

Just before it blinked out, he saw a vast horned shadow on the wall.

# 26

The bull walked around the corner into the passage where Hylas stood frozen with horror. Taller than the tallest man, its dark bulk loomed before him. He breathed its hot rank smell. He took a step back.

The bull halted.

Hylas took another step back. The roof beams above him were too high to reach, and if he made a run for it, he'd be trampled to death.

Suddenly he became aware of a glimmer of light behind the bull. "Don't move," said Pirra's voice from the gloom. A moment later, he saw her. In one hand she held a rush-light, in the other, a length of yellow silk.

At the sound of her voice, the bull swung around, its horns raking chunks of plaster off the walls. Pirra twitched the silk past its nose and disappeared the way she'd come. The bull threw down its head and clattered after her.

"*Run!*" she yelled.

But Hylas wasn't going to let her face a monster on her own, and he raced after them: around the corner, down a ramp, through a big pair of bronze-studded doors flung wide and out into a vast, dim hall.

In a heartbeat he took in twin ranks of tall red columns supporting shadowy balconies, and a lamp at the far end, before a giant double axe of hammered gold. The floor was spattered with bull's droppings; the smell hung thick in the air. Then he saw Pirra dodging behind a column, trailing the silk, with the infuriated bull in hot pursuit.

Hylas rushed toward them, waving his arms, shouting, "Here! After me!" But the bull was intent on Pirra. She fled for the next column, dropping the silk behind her. The beast trampled it and came on. She reached the column and ducked behind it. With startling agility the bull swerved to cut her off, the tip of one horn missing her thigh by a whisker.

"Here! Here!" yelled Hylas—but still the bull lunged at Pirra, trapping her behind the column.

Hylas put his hands to his mouth and howled like a wolf.

That got the bull's attention, and it spun around, pawing the floor. Which of these infuriating humans should it attack—and where was the wolf?

Again Hylas howled. The bull flung up its head and *bellowed*. The ground shook and the great hall echoed with the roars of a hundred bulls.

Meanwhile, Pirra had seized her chance to escape: Hylas saw her making for some shadowy stairs halfway down the hall. The stairs were too narrow for the bull: If she reached them, she could climb to safety.

The bull had seen her; she wasn't going to make it.

Suddenly out of the dark swooped a bolt of black lightning. It was Echo, skimming low over the bull's back, then twisting around for another go. Enraged by this fresh intruder, the bull turned this way and that. Echo dived perilously low, drew in her wings at the last moment, and sped right between its front legs. Then she glided off and perched with a ringing *eck-eck* between the golden blades of the giant double axe.

For one frozen heartbeat, Pirra stared fixedly at the falcon on the axe; then she glanced back at Hylas. The bull was between them, he couldn't reach the stairs.

"You go!" he shouted. "I'll be all right!"

She vanished up the stairs and he raced back for the doorway—but the bull came thundering after him.

"Hylas!" yelled Pirra from somewhere behind. "There's a beam in the passage!"

A beam? What did she mean? The bull was gaining on him, he could hear its grunting breath.

*There's a beam in the passage . . . Of course.* Hurtling out of the hall, Hylas grabbed the brass-studded doors and swung them shut with a clang. He groped in the dark— found the beam propped against the wall—and dropped it in place, barring the doors the instant before the bull crashed into them.

The great doors of Kunisu shuddered, but held fast.

As Hylas leaned panting against the wall, he heard a furious bellow from the hall; then the diminishing clop of hooves as the bull trotted off—and finally a huffing snort that sounded not angry, but satisfied.

The bull had seen off the intruders, and regained possession of its domain.

———

"What were you *doing* over here?" cried Pirra when she found Hylas on his knees outside the Hall of the Double Axe.

"I got lost," he panted. "And I didn't expect to meet a giant bull! I thought—did it come out of the walls?"

"Of course not! The priests must've left it to guard Kunisu."

"And you didn't think to *tell* me?" he exploded.

"All I knew was that they might have left some kind of guardian, I didn't know it was a bull! What *were* you doing wandering about in the understory in the dark? I woke up and found you gone, I looked all over!"

"I told you, I got lost!"

She'd dropped her rushlight in the Hall, but in the gloom she saw that he was shaking. So was she. She was furious with him for scaring her like that—and appalled by Echo's sudden appearance in the Hall. The image of the falcon perched on the sacred double axe was seared on her mind. It was surely no chance that Echo had alighted there. It was a sign from the Goddess.

"Well anyway, thanks," muttered Hylas. "If you hadn't come, I'd have been finished."

She swallowed. "Next time you wander off, *wake* me. Or maybe I should do what Userref used to do when I was little, and tie a thread to my bedpost and the other end round your wrist; that way, you *can't* get lost."

He snorted a laugh. Then he said, "But you know what this means? Userref can't be here, or he'd have heard us shouting and come running. It'll be dawn soon, let's clear out. Can you find your room in the dark?"

"Hylas, I've lived here my whole life, I could find my way blindfolded."

They emerged into the Great Court as the sky was getting light. Pirra quickened her pace, uneasily aware of all the times her mother had performed public sacrifices out here.

Hylas asked what they should do about the bull. "We can't just leave it down there."

How like Hylas, she thought with a pang, to think about that. "The priests will have left it water and hay," she said. "Sooner or later they'll come and let it out."

At that moment, she heard the faint rearrangement of air that told her Echo was near, and an instant later, the falcon settled on her shoulder.

For a moment, Echo's great dark eye met hers, and Pirra felt a jolt of meaning course through her. "I understand," she told the falcon quietly.

Echo shook out her wings with a snap, then took a lock of Pirra's hair and drew it gently through her beak.

"That bird's mad," said Hylas. "Did you see her fly between its legs?"

"She—she was just practicing flying," muttered Pirra.

He caught something in her tone and gave her a curious glance. "Down in that hall, there was a lamp burning in front of the axe. Was it you who lit it?"

"Yes. When I was looking for you."

"Why?"

"Because—because I had a question that needed answering."

"Did it work?"

"Yes."

They reached the East Stairs, and Hylas touched her shoulder. "That's the way to the balcony above the river, yes? We should go up and check it's still clear of Crows."

"You go," said Pirra, "I'll wait here." She couldn't face the Ridge of the Dead, or the stone eye of her mother's tomb.

"Are you all right?" said Hylas.

"Fine. This time, don't get lost."

As he took the stairs two at a time, Pirra slumped on the bottom one and hugged her knees to stop them shaking.

There was no escaping it now. She'd asked for a sign, and the Goddess had sent her the clearest one of all: Echo perched on one of the most sacred objects in Kunisu.

Pirra knew now what she had to do. The only question was whether she had the courage.

Footsteps above her, and Hylas came flying down the stairs. "They're down by the river," he whispered, grabbing her wrist and dragging her to her feet. "We've got to get out of here!"

When they reached her room, he rushed about gathering their gear. He noticed that she wasn't helping. "Hurry up!"

"You go," she told him. "I have to stay."

He stared at her. "*What?*"

"I can't go with you, Hylas. I have to stay here."

"But the Crows—"

"I know. But I have to perform the Mystery. There's no one else but me."

# 27

"You can't," said Hylas. "The Crows are going to break in at any moment."

"That's *why* I've got to do it," said Pirra. "I'll never get another chance."

"But Pirra there's no *time!*"

"And if the Sun doesn't come back, there'll be famine, and no time for any of us!"

He stared at her. "You really mean to do this."

"And I have to do it alone, Hylas. You need to get out while you can."

"What, and leave you here by yourself?"

"I know Kunisu, the Crows don't. I can hide for long enough to . . . Hylas please! Do this for me." Now that she'd made up her mind, she was desperate for him to leave. Every moment he stayed made it harder.

He glanced at the slingshot in his hands, then back to her. "Why do *you* have to do it? What about all those priests—"

"They're men. It has to be a priestess—"

"Which you're not!"

"No, but I'm Yassassara's daughter and I know what to do. There's no time to explain, but I know—in here"—she struck her heart with her fist—"that I have to do what my mother would have done if she'd lived. If you want to help me, you have to go!"

He gave her a long searching look. Then his mouth set in a stubborn line. "No. I meant what I said in the mountains. We won't be separated again."

Pirra drew a breath. "This is different."

*"Why?"*

She couldn't tell him. If he knew, he'd never let her do it.

"No," he said again. "I'm not leaving you. I'll keep the Crows at bay while you do whatever it is you have to do—then we're getting out of here. Together."

⸺

Pirra halted before the double doors of the High Priestess' innermost chamber. Her heart thudded against her breastbone and the rushlight trembled in her fist.

The doors creaked open at her touch. Outside, the dim gray day had dawned, but the chamber before her was dark. She had never been inside. She dreaded seeing Yassassara's ghost warding her back.

*Don't* think about Hylas, she told herself as she shut the doors behind her. But she couldn't help it. He'd told her he was going to set traps for the Crows, and she'd given him hasty directions for finding his way, then they'd parted at the foot of the stairs. So fast. No time to say good-bye.

Don't think about him—or Havoc or Echo. They're behind you now. They're in the past.

Once, she'd seen her mother perform a Mystery, but that had been a far lesser one than this. What she was about to attempt was unlike all other rites. There would be no bull-leaping, no sacrifice of ox or ram, and no watching crowd. This Mystery came from ancient times, when the gods had demanded human life.

She made out a brazier set for a fire, and touched it with the rushlight. Flames leaped, and with a jolt, she saw that everything for the Mystery had been laid out, waiting for her.

The green glass bowl of frankincense, the ivory dishes of ground earth, the rock-crystal phials of sacred oils . . . She realized that on the other side of Kunisu, she would find another brazier on the West Balcony, and the alabaster conch shell for summoning the Goddess.

With a thrill of horror, Pirra stared at the rich robes of Keftian purple laid out on the chest. They still bore the shape of her mother's body. Perhaps Yassassara had been about to begin when the Plague had struck her down—or perhaps she had foreseen that her daughter would stand here now.

Suddenly, Pirra's spirit rebelled. I don't have to do this! I don't even know if I *can*! Why should I forfeit my life if

I don't even know it'll work? I'm not going to, I'm going to find Hylas and run away . . .

And then what? said the other part of her mind. Hide out somewhere and watch Keftiu wither and die?

Again she saw the child in the cavern, eking out her last days in hunger and despair.

Setting her teeth, Pirra filled the porphyry basin with seawater from the jar, then hurriedly stripped and washed. Her teeth chattered as she twisted gold wire in her hair and piled it in coils on her head, leaving seven locks snaking down.

In each ivory dish, she mixed oils of hyacinth and myrrh with powders ground from stones of different hues, then painted herself all over: white gypsum on her face and body, red ochre on her palms and the soles of her feet. There. That was for the earth of Keftiu.

For the Sea, she donned Yassassara's heavy skirt of Keftian purple and her tight, open-breasted bodice. She tied her waist with the sacred knot of Sea silk, spun from the red-gold filaments of giant mussels. She sprinkled her robes with oil of Sea lily, and tried not to think about why her bodice bared the heart: to take the knife.

For the sky, she put on anklets, earrings, and wristcuffs incised with sacred birds. With trembling hands, she placed her mother's great collar of the Sun about her neck, where it lay heavy and chill against her flesh.

Already the gypsum was stiffening on her face, and

when she touched her cheek, she couldn't feel her scar. The earth of Keftiu had hidden it and rendered her perfect, as befitted a vessel for the Goddess.

From downstairs came a muffled squawk that she recognized as Echo—followed by Hylas' voice, sounding annoyed. She shut her eyes. Don't think about them. He'll look after Echo. He'll teach her to hunt.

Taking a brush made of the tip of a squirrel's tail and trying not to meet her gaze in her mother's bronze mirror, she painted her eyelids with henna and poppy juice— so that she might see with the eyes of the Goddess. She painted the tips of her ears red—that she might hear with the ears of the Goddess, and her lips—that she might speak with the voice of the Goddess.

She hesitated. Only one thing missing now.

The ebony box lay open to reveal the knife. It was silver, the blade enamelled with a blue dolphin leaping over black waves. Pirra didn't want to touch it. When she did, she would be ready: to descend to the Hall of Whispers and twine the sacred snakes about her arms, and wake the gods of the underworld . . .

To cross the Great Court and climb to the Upper Chamber and burn frankincense for the gods of the sky . . .

Last of all, to blow the alabaster conch shell and beg the Goddess to bring back the Sun: to raise the knife and complete the Mystery . . .

Footsteps echoed as Hylas came running upstairs.

Pirra took the knife and slid it into the gilded sheath at her hip. Make him pass without stopping. Don't let me see him, or I won't have the strength to go through with this.

He stopped outside the double doors. They creaked as he pushed them open.

"Hylas don't—" she said over her shoulder.

It wasn't Hylas.

It was Telamon.

# 28

For a heartbeat, Telamon thought one of the painted goddesses had stepped down from the walls.

Then he saw that it was Pirra—and yet not Pirra: an alien priestess in a tight open-breasted bodice and flowing skirts the color of crushed grapes. Gold snakes coiled in her hair, and her flesh glittered eerily white. Her black eyes regarded him coldly, without fear. He didn't dare touch her. And he knew that she knew it too.

"You don't belong here," she said levelly. "Get out while you still can."

The power in her voice made his skin prickle. "I came for what's mine," he croaked. "Give me the dagger."

She spread her hands, and from her skirts rose a dizzying fragrance. "I don't have it," she said.

"I don't believe you."

"I don't care. Get out while you can. *Crow.*"

He bridled. "I'm the grandson of Koronos, my blood's as good as yours."

Her red lips curved in a smile that made his face burn. "You're an Akean," she said. "We Keftians were pouring libations in the Great Court when you were still living in caves."

"Hylas is Akean too," he said.

"And isn't it odd? He's a goatherd, you're a chieftain's son—and yet he's all that's best in Akea, and you're all that's worst." Her glance flicked to his wrist, where her sealstone hung beside his; then to the gold plaques on his belt, which had once been hers. "You Crows know how to chop things up, but you can't create."

"We know how to conquer," he retorted. "You Keftians can't even defend yourselves! It only took two of my men to scale the wall and open the gates."

If she was dismayed, she hid it well. "Poor Telamon," she said with mock pity. "Do you imagine that you can conquer us with *warriors*? Kunisu has stood since the dawn of time! We have other ways of defending ourselves. Leave now, before you find out what they are."

His courage wavered. They'd found it suspiciously easy to break into the House of the Goddess, but once inside, they'd been unnerved by its twisting passages and walls that turned out to be screens masking sudden lethal drops; and by the dreadful bellowing of some underground monster.

"It's as if they don't *need* to keep us out," Kreon had muttered. "And now that we're inside . . ." Soon after, Telamon had lost his way and found himself alone. *Now that we're inside . . .*

From far off came shouts, the clash of weapons, then

silence. Pirra gave a start. She recovered fast, but the spell was broken.

She's no priestess, Telamon thought savagely. She's just a frightened girl. "I've had enough of your tricks," he snarled. "I want the dagger and I want Hylas, now!"

"No," she said. But her shoulders were high, and he saw a vein beating in her throat.

"Why defend him?" he demanded. "What's he to you?" He wanted to grab her shoulders and shake her. Can't you see that I'm better than him? Stronger, handsomer, richer! How *dare* you prefer him to me!

"It's over, Pirra," he said. "I've won. My men will search every corner till they find him. Give me the dagger and I won't hurt you—but forget about Hylas. There's nothing you can do for him now."

—❦—

Pirra forced herself to meet his gaze. Then, very deliberately, she turned her back on him.

She felt his eyes on her as she touched a reed to the brazier, then to the frankincense in the green glass bowl. Would he guess that she was playing for time—racking her brains for some means of escape, while straining her ears for some hint that Hylas had gotten away?

"Give me the dagger," repeated Telamon.

As the frankincense caught, an idea came to her. It was horribly risky, but there was no other way. With the bowl in both hands, she faced him. "What will you do if I don't?"

Telamon's eyes narrowed. With his cloak flung back and

his dagger in his fist, he looked terrifyingly strong. She would never outrun him, or get a chance to draw the silver knife at her hip. Her only weapon was his unease.

In the green glass bowl, flames licked the little crystalline lumps of the sacred resin, sending up twisting threads of sour black smoke. Pirra blew them out, and instantly the smoke turned white, as she'd known it would, and the chamber filled with the astonishing perfume of frankincense. "What will you do?" she repeated softly.

Telamon rearranged his fingers on his dagger. His face was flushed, and beads of sweat stood out on his upper lip.

Holding the bowl before her so that he saw her through the perfumed haze, Pirra backed deeper into the chamber.

He came after her. "Oh no, don't think you can run away."

"I'm not," she replied. "You are in the forbidden chamber of the High Priestess. It's you who should run away."

By the brazier's dying glow, she saw him take in the painted goddesses on the walls, making sacrifices and summoning hawks and lions to do their will. She took another step back. Behind her were three doorways, each hidden behind a hanging embroidered in poisonous greens and stinging yellows. All opened onto a dark windowless passage where gaps in the parapet showed glimpses of a shadowy corner of Kunisu, two stories below.

Telamon's eyes darted in alarm from one door to the next.

"What's behind these doors?" said Pirra in a low voice.

"What Keftian magic lies in wait for the intruder?"

"You can't frighten me," he muttered.

She forced a smile. "But you are frightened. No man may enter here." She passed the smoking bowl before his face, and he recoiled with a gasp. "Did you think we'd leave Kunisu unprotected?" she whispered. "The Goddess won't forgive you for this!"

He lifted his chin. "I'm not afraid. Your Goddess has abandoned Keftiu. And I have the favor of the Angry Ones."

"Then where are they? All Keftiu is covered in ash, and yet the Angry Ones are nowhere—because my mother banished them! Her magic is vastly stronger than your spirits!"

"Yassassara's dead," he said thickly.

"But her spells live on." She wafted another gust of frankincense in his face, and as he drew back, she seized her chance and fled: through the middle doorway and into the dimness beyond.

With a shout Telamon came after her, as she'd hoped he would. Swiftly she side-stepped, but he blundered ahead, didn't see the gap in the parapet—and stepped out onto empty air.

He made no sound as he fell, but she heard the thud as he hit the ground. Setting the bowl on the parapet, she leaned over.

Telamon sprawled on the stones below. He wasn't moving. Pirra couldn't tell if he was injured or dead. As she breathed in the frankincense, it seemed to cut her loose from herself, so that she felt neither guilt nor remorse. "I warned you," she said.

Picking up the bowl, she returned to the chamber. She set the bowl on the table and took the silver pitcher her mother's priests had put ready, and filled the obsidian goblet with poppy juice and pomegranate wine.

She drank. She was no longer Pirra. She was a vessel for the Shining One.

Lighting another rushlight, she opened the double doors and started for the Hall of Whispers, to begin the Mystery.

# 29

The boy, the girl, and even that wretched falcon had been swallowed by this great horned mountain—and only the lion cub was left outside.

She felt a bit battered after falling out of the tree, and she limped as she prowled the mountain's feet. From somewhere within came the cries of that stupid bird. It sounded as if it was in trouble. Well, good. It wasn't *fair* that the falcon was inside with the boy, just because she could fly.

Darkness gaped in the mountain's flank, and the lion cub halted. She was back before those dreadful gaping jaws that had swallowed the boy and girl—and what was worse, they now reeked of the terrible men with the flying black hides who had killed her parents.

Flattening her ears, the cub hunkered down to think. *No no no,* she couldn't go in there.

But the terrible men were hunting the boy.

In an agony of terror, the cub flexed her claws in and out. She couldn't go in there, not even for him.

But he needed her.

The lion cub twitched her tail and tightened her haunches. Then she seized her courage in her jaws and darted inside.

~~~

The falcon was exhausted, frightened, and *angry*. It was her own fault that she'd gotten herself trapped.

After saving the girl from the bull, the falcon had flown off to find a roost in a nice dark corner of one of the caves. Some time later, she'd woken with a sense that the girl was in trouble again. The falcon didn't know how she felt this, but she did, to the roots of her feathers.

So once again she'd sped through the narrow winding caves. She'd forgotten all about those giant cobwebs that spanned the caves—until it was too late, and she crashed into one.

The cobweb was tougher than it looked, and although the falcon pecked and lashed out with her talons, she couldn't tear herself free. She'd been struggling for ages, but the more she fought, the more tangled up she became.

Now her wings were squeezed shut and she couldn't move a claw. It was awful, like being back in the Egg.

~~~

It was awful inside the mountain.

The ground was menacingly smooth beneath the lion cub's paws, and on either side of her rose strange threatening trees with very straight trunks that she didn't dare scratch.

At times, she blundered into giant cobwebs spanning

the mouths of caves. They clung unpleasantly to her muzzle, and she had to claw herself free with both forepaws.

Worst of all, everywhere stank of the bad humans. The caves were so echoey that the cub couldn't tell where they were, but she heard their yowls and the clash of their long shiny claws.

At last she caught the boy's scent and followed it to a pile of dead sheep. She smelled that he'd curled up on them and had one of his endless sleeps, and this made her feel a bit braver.

Nosing a sheep, she was startled to find that it was nothing but pelt, with no meat inside. She ripped open the smallest, fattest sheep, and to her astonishment, it was full of feathers. What kind of sheep has feathers instead of guts?

Coughing and sneezing, the lion cub forgot about the empty sheep and padded into the next cave, which smelled strongly of the boy and the girl. They weren't here now, but they'd left her some meat, so she settled down to eat, swiveling her ears for the least sound of the terrible men.

Somewhere not far off, that falcon was squawking again. Let her squawk. Hungrily, the lion cub gulped more meat.

---

The falcon struggled, but it was no use; the cobwebs held her fast—and now some earthbound monster was coming toward her.

Helpless as a sparrow, the falcon lay with her beak agape and her heart fluttering in her breast. She saw the enormous shadow drawing close. She heard harsh sawing breath.

A huge black nose nudged her roughly in the breast—
and sniffed.

———

The lion cub sniffed the falcon and patted her with one
forepaw.

The falcon hissed, but she couldn't move: The giant
cobweb held her fast. With her wings squeezed shut, she
looked even punier than usual. The cub thought about
eating her, but she was mostly feathers and wouldn't make
a mouthful. Besides, the lion cub was full, and feathers
made her sneeze.

Again she patted the falcon, who glared at her as she
swung back and forth in the cobweb. The cub did it again,
but this time the cobweb snagged her claws, so she ripped
them free, and the falcon fell to the ground with a thud.

Curious, the lion cub batted the bird between her forepaws. The falcon shrieked and lashed out with one foot,
catching the lion cub a painful scratch on her pad.

The cub snarled. The falcon hissed.

Suddenly the lion cub heard men yowling, alarmingly
close.

The falcon flew off. The cub fled in terror. The caves
were so echoey that she couldn't tell if the bad humans
were ahead or behind. She wished she'd followed the
falcon—at least then she wouldn't be alone.

Where were the bad humans?

And where was the boy?

# 30

Echo swept past Hylas and he nearly fell off the ladder, which angered the wasps, who buzzed furiously around his head. One stung his ear and another his thumb. Clenching his jaw, he tied the cord around the wasps' nest, then slid down the ladder, looped the cord at ankle height around the pillars on either side of the passage, and raced off. There. Another trap set.

As yet, he'd seen no sign of the Crows, but he knew it wouldn't be long. Earlier, he'd peered out of a window and glimpsed a black swarm of them at the north gates. He'd counted twenty-two, including Telamon and Kreon. Twenty-two against one. He didn't want to think about that.

If he'd been out in the wild, he would have made boulders into deadfalls and saplings into spring-loaded spikes. In here, his only plan was to frighten them off. In a workshop he'd thrown together a couple of lumpy wax figures, and sloshed water in powdered lime to make runny white paint; then he'd raced about, leaving the pus-eaters where they'd look most menacing, and marking doors with the white handprints of Plague.

If that didn't work and it came to a fight, he was finished. All he had were axe, knife, and slingshot—with not enough shot, just a pouchful of big carnelian beads from a necklace of Pirra's.

As he ran, he felt a stab of worry at leaving her alone. She was somewhere in the east of Kunisu, while he was in the west, with the Great Court between them. Although no one knew better how to hide in here than Pirra, if the Crows caught her, he wouldn't even hear her scream.

Turning a corner, he started down a shadowy passage flanked by workshops. No handprints on the doors; he hadn't set any traps here. He bumped into a brazier and sent it clattering, then tripped over a coil of rope. That'd come in handy; he slung it over his shoulder.

At the end of the passage, torchlight glimmered. Hylas crouched behind the brazier. Any moment now and Crow warriors would appear around the corner.

Torchlight glimmered at the *other* end too. The Crows were approaching the passage from both ends.

In panic, Hylas threw himself into the nearest workshop. Please please don't let it be a dead end.

It was. No windows, no ceiling hatch, not even a drain to crawl into. Just a dim chamber cluttered with tools.

"Search every room!" shouted a man from one end of the passage. The crash of breaking pottery: The two parties of Crows were working their way toward each other, ransacking every workshop as they went. The one where Hylas hid was in the middle. It wouldn't be long before they found him.

In panic, he cast about him. On a workbench he saw three of those weird giant eggs; no use to him.

The din was getting nearer.

He backed deeper into the gloom, and something jabbed his shoulder blade. It was one of those giant tusks; in fact, a whole wobbly stack of them.

The Crows were almost upon him.

In feverish haste, he tied a loop in one end of his rope and slung it over a tusk jutting from the middle of the stack; then, placing a giant egg on the floor to distract the Crows, he darted behind the workbench, gripping the other end of the rope in both hands.

An instant later, the room filled with the stench of sweat and the creak of rawhide armor. Torchlight slid across the floor toward him.

"Told you there's no one here," growled a man, shockingly close. "I say we get out before we catch Plague."

"Those handprints were fresh, you idiot!" snapped another. "Who d'you think made them?"

"I don't care! This whole place feels cursed, I'm getting out!"

Mutters of agreement from the others, but the one who'd noticed the paint didn't back down. "You heard the orders," he insisted, "check every cubit!"

The torchlight slid closer to Hylas' foot. He fought the urge to recoil, knowing that the slightest move would betray him.

"What's *that*?"

He froze.

"Looks like—a giant *egg*."

"Don't touch it, it's cursed."

"What's that over there?"

The torchlight moved even closer. With a desperate prayer to the Lady of the Wild Things, Hylas yanked the rope as hard as he could. The pile of tusks tottered—and fell with a crash.

Torches went flying, men shouted and swore in the dark. Seizing his chance, Hylas scrambled past them and out the door.

The Crows recovered terrifyingly fast. As he sped down the passage, shouts rang out. "There he is!"

He hurtled around the bend, slipped on a rug, and staggered past a doorway flanked by two painted lions with wings. He'd seen them before: He'd set another trap somewhere close.

This time, he let the Crows catch a glimpse of him.

"That way!" one yelled.

They were so intent on catching him that they didn't see the rope at ankle height. He heard the lead warriors go down in a clatter of weapons, then men howling in rage and pain as the wasps' nest burst.

A swarm of furious wasps wouldn't delay them for long. Hylas found a stairway that he recognized and sped up it, past a lumpy little pus-eater that glared at him from the bottom step with red carnelian eyes.

He'd scarcely reached the dark at the top when warriors appeared at the foot. They saw the pus-eater and lurched to a halt.

"Told you this place is cursed," panted one.

"Whatever you saw, it can't have been human," whispered another. "I'm getting out!"

This time, no one argued.

Shaking with relief, Hylas listened to them go. From a window on an upper gallery, he saw them streaming out of the gates. He counted nine, far better than he'd dared hope. Now the odds were only thirteen against one.

It was getting hotter. Yanking his jerkin over his head, he stuffed it behind a brazier and headed off.

Downstairs, he found himself in another endless passage, with giant earthenware jars standing sentinel between workshops along one side. All the doors except one bore his white handprints.

More torchlight and creaking armor. He darted into the one room that bore no handprint. This time, he *wanted* the Crows to give the Plague-marked workshops only a cursory look, and concentrate on his hiding place: It was his final trap. Either that, or it would be his tomb.

The room was dark, and full of an eye-watering stink. Dung crunched underfoot and he fought the urge to gag as he slipped behind the column by the door and climbed onto its base, so that his face was near the roof beams. They were thick with sleeping bats, hanging motionless. Across the room, he made out the pale rectangle of the opposite door, which earlier he'd left ajar, with a basket balanced on top.

"He went in there, I saw him," a warrior said hoarsely.

Light glimmered in the workshop, but the bats slept on. Hylas watched in horrified fascination as warriors passed within touching distance of the column behind which he hid. He heard the hiss of their pine-pitch torches. He saw the sweat beading their muscles and the vicious gleam of spears. If they found him, he'd be skewered like a pike.

It was time to put his plan to the test. The surest way to waken bats is to mimic their worst enemy. Putting his mouth close to the cluster near his face, Hylas *hissed*.

Snakes invaded the bats' dark dreams, and the colony exploded in twittering panic. Shouting in disgust and clawing at bats, the warriors fled for the opposite door, bringing down the basket with its load of whipsnakes. Torches went flying, men roared and trampled each other.

"Told you this place is cursed," yelled one. "I'm getting out!"

"Orders is orders, you can't run away, you coward!"

A torrent of oaths—and now bronze was clashing with bronze, the Crows were fighting each other. In the lurching light, Hylas saw a man fall, clutching his belly. Another crumpled with blood bubbling from his mouth. The coppery tang caught at Hylas' throat, and he smelled the stink of burst bowels. The bats and snakes had fled: He followed their lead and slipped unnoticed into the passage. If he was lucky, the Crows would slaughter each other, and those who survived would flee.

Which still left a handful unaccounted for, including Kreon and Telamon. Somehow, he had to get back to the staircase where he'd left Pirra.

But now he found himself running down a passage he'd never seen before. It was painted a burning yellow, and its floor was set with red river pebbles, knobbly and painful under his bare feet.

He stumbled into an enormous hall that was also unfamiliar. He saw black ivy painted on the walls and oxblood hangings stirring in a breeze. Benches and three-legged tables lay overturned on moldering rushes—as if the hall had only just been deserted by a gathering of ghosts.

Hylas cast about him. Which way? All the arches and doorways looked the same.

An arrow whined past his ear. He flung himself sideways, and cried out as another grazed his calf.

Grabbing a bench, he held it against him as a shield.

Above him on a balcony, he glimpsed a shadowy figure crouch to nock another arrow to its bow.

# 31

The lion cub heard the boy's cry and quickened her pace. He needed her, but this long narrow cave was so twisty and the smells were so tangled up, she couldn't *find* him.

She reached a place where the cave split in two, and halted. Which way?

As she snuffed the air, the falcon swept past and perched on a ledge. The lion cub flicked the bird an irritable look, which the falcon ignored.

Shaking out her wings, the bird lifted off again and disappeared around the bend. Ah. Maybe that way. The cub followed on silent pads.

Her hackles rose. The bad human crouched behind a ledge a few pounces away, shooting a long flying fang into the cave below. The lion cub smelled his blood-hunger. She sensed the boy's pain and fear wafting up from the cave. Soundlessly, she gathered herself for the spring.

Intent on the hunt, the bad human reached behind him for another flying fang. He didn't know she was there.

The cub sprang. With a howl, the bad human dropped

a bunch of flying fangs, which went clattering over the ledge. He was weak, but squirmier than she expected. She tried to bite his throat, but got his shoulder instead; it was surprisingly tough and tasted of ox-hide. Now he was scratching her muzzle with his forepaws and jamming his knee in her belly. For a tail flick her grip loosened. He twisted from under her and lashed out with a big shiny claw. The cub dodged, but again he lashed out, just missing her eye.

Snarling, she backed away. Snarling, the bad human lurched to his feet. Suddenly, two more bad humans came running to his aid. The lion cub turned tail and fled.

As she ran, she glanced down at the cave and saw the boy. He was limping but alive; she felt grimly satisfied. Those long flying fangs couldn't hurt him now.

The cries of the bad humans faded behind her, and she slowed to a trot. She smelled bats and blood, but she'd lost the boy's scent.

The falcon glided past and perched on a ledge, as if waiting for her to catch up. The cub ignored her—then relented, and acknowledged the bird with a flick of one ear.

Again the falcon flew past, and again waited for the cub to catch up. They reached the end of the long cave, and for the first time, bird and lion cub exchanged glances rather than glares. Then they went their separate ways: the cub to find the boy, and the falcon to seek the girl.

The lion cub felt that this was good. It was how things should be. Maybe the falcon had her uses after all.

# 32

Pirra had been in the Hall of Whispers forever, whirling and chanting in a cloud of incense. Words of power streamed behind her like smoke, cutting her off from the mortal world.

Against her thigh lay the silver knife that would soon sever her spirit. Before her rose the sacred horns and between them like a dark Moon hung the obsidian mirror that would reveal the face of the Goddess.

Incense, wine, and poppy juice had blunted her terror, but deep inside, the fierce bright kernel that remained Pirra fought to make out Hylas' voice from the distant clamor of fighting.

Still chanting, she uncovered the basket and drew out a snake in either hand. Heavy coils entwined her arms. She felt the tiny pinch of scales gripping her flesh, and narrow black tongues flicking out to taste her skin.

Still chanting, she grasped the sacrificial vessel of green serpentine shaped like a bull's head, and from its gilded muzzle poured a stream of wine in a vast dark spiral on the floor, moving inward until she stood at the heart of the vortex.

With a ringing shout, she uttered the final word of power, and shattered the bull's head on the stones. Even now, her spirit fluttered in a desperate bid for freedom—but the dark spiral sucked her down, then lifted her high in a blinding flash that scorched away terror, doubt, humanity. She stared into the obsidian mirror . . .

. . . and the Goddess stared back.

The girl named Pirra is gone. The face in the mirror is the Shining One: She Who Has Power.

Shards of serpentine are sharp beneath Her feet, but She feels no pain, for She is immortal. She will descend into the Underworld and release Her Brother the Earthshaker. She will ascend and summon Her Brother the Lord of the Sky, and together They will bring back the Sun. Then with the silver blade She will cut Her deathless spirit free from its mortal flesh . . .

Down, down She goes, and opens the doors of the Underworld. She calls to Her Brother the Earthshaker, who bows His mighty head and walks toward Her. She holds out Her hand, and His moist breath heats Her palm. With Her other hand on the matted hair between His horns, She bids Him go, and rid Keftiu of evil.

—

A bat flickered past Hylas as he limped down the passage. His calf throbbed where the arrow had grazed it, and he'd dropped his axe in the attack; he felt horribly vulnerable.

And he was worried about Havoc. He would never have

escaped if she hadn't attacked that archer—but had she gotten away unhurt? Where was she now?

And where was Pirra? A while back, he'd heard her chanting in the distance, then a shout—and silence. Was that part of the Mystery, or was she in trouble?

By his reckoning, there couldn't be many Crows left in Kunisu. The archer had fled with his companions, convinced that the place was full of man-eating beasts—but this still left Telamon and Kreon. What if they'd found Pirra? And how was he, Hylas, to find her, when he had no idea where he was?

Another bat flickered past, and he glimpsed a whipsnake disappearing down a drain. Turning a corner, he found himself in a passage with doors stretching ahead, each marked with a handprint, except one. Hylas' spirit shrank. He was back where he'd sprung his final trap and the Crows had fought each other.

As he limped closer, he smelled blood and saw dead warriors slumped in the doorway. Waxy fists clutched bloodied weapons and he caught a snaky gleam of entrails.

He fled, not caring where he went, and from the tail of his eye he saw a ghostly warrior sit up and stare with hollow eyes.

Hylas lurched around a corner, careening into a huge jar that toppled with a crash.

Ghostly footsteps echoed. It was coming after him.

He blundered into a screen, clawed his way through a silk hanging, then another that rattled like bones.

Still the footsteps came on.

At last he had to pause, bent double and gasping for air. The thing was still following—but now he heard *breath*. What stalked him was no ghost; it was a living man, pursuing him with the steady tread of a warrior intent on his prey.

In panic, Hylas shouldered open the nearest door—and burst out into the shocking daylight of the Great Court.

He saw the sacred olive tree at its heart and the giant double axe at the north end that guarded the ramp to the understory. On all sides, painted crowds stared back at him with silent scorn. Wherever he turned, the doors were barred. With a sensation of falling, he knew he was trapped in this naked space where there was nowhere to hide.

From the doorway he'd just fled walked a warrior. With unhurried ease he shut the doors behind him, and turned to face Hylas.

"At last," said Kreon.

# 33

I n the ashen light of the Great Court, the Crow Chieftain looked enormous.

His boar's-tusk helmet could turn any blade, and his
armor was thick rawhide and impenetrable bronze. His
shield was studded ox-hide as tall as a man, but he bore it
lightly on one shoulder as if it was birch bark. He moved
with the swagger of a hunter sure of his prey: a seasoned
killer armed with sword, spear, dagger, and whip. Hylas
was a boy of thirteen with a knife, a slingshot, and a bag
of beads.

As Hylas drew his knife, Kreon's whip cracked out,
yanked it from his fist, and sent it skittering over the
stones. The whip struck again. Hylas leaped sideways. Not
fast enough. He yelped as its bronze tip bit his thigh.

Again and again the whip forced him back toward the
empty heart of the Great Court. The only weapon that
could help him was the giant double axe, hopelessly out of
reach at the north end—with Kreon in the way. In desper-
ation, Hylas dodged behind the sacred tree.

"That's not going to work," sneered Kreon.

Hylas fumbled at his pouch and grabbed a bead for his slingshot. The carnelian slipped through his fingers and bounced over the stones. He loaded another and swung the slingshot at Kreon's face. The warrior parried it with his shield—and the next shot and the next.

"Is that all you've got?" Kreon grinned as he drove Hylas around and around the tree. One by one, Hylas' shots clanged off ox-hide and bronze. Suddenly he had only three left.

His first struck Kreon's kneecap; the warrior didn't even blink. The second hit his wrist bone with a crack that made him drop his spear with a hiss. As he stooped to retrieve it, Hylas took aim with his final shot. He'd saved the biggest for last, and a stone the size of a pigeon's egg hit Kreon on the throat. The warrior gave a choking roar, but recovered fast, and charged.

Dropping the slingshot, Hylas fled, zigzagging toward the double axe on its mount. For a big man, Kreon moved with terrifying speed, but Hylas was faster. Grabbing the axe shaft with both hands, he pulled. It was sunk deep in its mount; it wouldn't come out. Kreon was almost upon him. With a last gut-straining heave, Hylas wrenched the axe free. It was so heavy he nearly fell over, but some-how he swung it, missing Kreon and striking the stones instead. Kreon jabbed with his sword. Hylas leaped side-ways, swung the axe again, and brought it down with shat-tering force on Kreon's shield.

Undaunted, the warrior cast off the mangled ox-hide

and came at Hylas again, feinting this way and that with sword and whip. Struggling with the weight of the axe, Hylas edged backward. Behind him lay the dark ramp leading down to the understory: His only way out.

But no sooner had he formed the thought than Kreon guessed, and moved behind to cut him off. Once again, his whip forced Hylas back to the unprotected heart of the Great Court.

Hylas was exhausted. The yellow stone floor with its painted blue leaves swam before his eyes, and the axe was a dead weight, a lethal hindrance in close combat. Kreon wasn't even breathing hard. Like any skilled hunter, he was making his quarry do the running.

As he closed in for the kill, he studied Hylas, and his heavy face twisted in scorn. "Can *this* be the Outsider who threatens the House of Koronos?"

"If you believe the Oracle," panted Hylas.

"Oracles!" spat Kreon. "Give me the dagger of Koronos, *boy*, and I'll give you an easy death."

"I haven't got it."

"I can see that. Take me to it, and I'll make it quick."

"No."

The Crow Chieftain was so close that Hylas could smell the rancid oil in his beard and see a thread of spittle stretched between his yellow teeth. "Listen to me, Outsider. You're going to die. The only question is how. Give me the dagger and you won't suffer. Refuse, and I'll make it last all day."

Hylas swayed.

"I'll make you long for death," Kreon went on. "I'll make you beg me to bring your suffering to an end . . ."

He was enjoying this. Hylas saw the red veins in the whites of his eyes, and the lightless pits of his pupils. Hylas thought of the men, women, and children who had perished in the mines of Thalakrea to satisfy this man's hunger for bronze. He thought how that hunger had angered the gods into bringing death and destruction to Keftiu. And he thought of his sister, who was either dead or battling to survive in the wilds of Messenia—because the Crows hunted Outsiders like beasts.

"My name," he panted, "isn't Outsider. It's Hylas. And I'll never give you the dagger."

Kreon looked at him. Then he nodded. "You've made your choice. Outsider."

His whip cracked out, but already Hylas was swinging his axe. It came down awkwardly, the flat of the blade missing Kreon's skull and dealing him a bone-crunching blow on the sword hand. Kreon bellowed and his sword went flying—but with the speed of a snake, he switched his whip to his injured hand and yanked his knife from his belt with the other.

Hylas dropped the axe and sped for the sacred tree. Reaching it just before his attacker, he clawed earth from its roots and flung it in Kreon's face. For an instant the warrior was blinded, and Hylas fled for the safety of the understory.

Halfway there, he spotted Kreon's spear on the ground and swerved to retrieve it. Mistake. The warrior's whip caught his ankle and jerked him off his feet.

For a heartbeat, Hylas' breath was knocked from his body, he couldn't move. He saw the spear lying just out of reach. He saw Kreon closing in for the kill.

As he struggled to his knees, Hylas caught movement on the ramp. Then a deafening bellow rent the air, hooves clattered on stone . . .

. . . and out from the understory galloped the guardian bull of Kunisu.

# 34

The wild bull thundered into the Great Court, then pawed the stones and swung its head, debating which human to attack first.

Hylas and Kreon stood frozen with shock. Then at the same moment they lunged for the spear on the ground. Hylas got it, but this caught the bull's attention and it charged.

Gripping the spear, Hylas ran. He saw Kreon step smartly out of the way. He heard the bull panting, and caught a jolting glimpse of one huge horn. It flashed across his mind that he couldn't outrun it and wasn't strong enough to fight it, not even with the spear. Mustering every shred of courage, he turned and ran *toward* it.

For an instant he met its white-rimmed eye, then he jammed the butt of the spear on the stones and vaulted over its back. At least he tried to, but his wobbly leap fell short, and he landed smack on its bony rump and slithered off in a heap.

With an outraged roar, the bull veered around and came at him again. Hylas scrambled to his feet. The bull guessed which way he'd go; its horn just missed his thigh. The spear had gone flying when Hylas fell, and as he raced across the Great Court, he saw Kreon grab it. Caught between an angry bull and a murderous warrior: He wasn't going to last much longer.

An echoing boom split the air—and the startled bull jolted to a halt. Kreon froze with the spear in his fist. It sounded like a ram's horn, only deeper, surging and receding like the Sea; and when the booming ceased, the echoes rang in Hylas' ears. He'd heard that sound before, two summers ago. Pirra had blown the alabaster conch shell to summon the gods.

The bull seemed to have mistaken it for the bellows of a rival bull, and was casting about with angry snorts. Kreon wasn't so easily distracted: He was circling the beast to get at Hylas.

Hylas staggered backward, trying to keep the bull between them. Suddenly the familiar pain stabbed his temple— no no no, not now—but this time instead of seeing ghosts, his senses turned preternaturally sharp. He heard lice sucking the blood inside the bull's ears, and a spider spinning a web in the sacred tree. He caught the hiss of Echo's wings as she soared far out of sight.

He saw Pirra.

She stood high above him on the West Balcony, and with a clutch of terror, he knew that she was utterly changed. She wore the purple open-breasted garb of the High Priestess, and living snakes entwined her naked arms.

Gold glinted at her throat and in the black coils of her hair, and she moved in a dreadful shimmering brightness. Her face was alight with a terrible radiance, and as she lifted her arms, her shadow on the wall grew vast, and burned with the fury of a thousand fires. In the deathless voice of an immortal, she cried out to the sky—and although Hylas couldn't understand, he knew that the Shining One was calling back the Sun.

All this took less than a heartbeat, then everything happened at once. Hylas saw the silver knife in her fist and understood what she meant to do. "*No Pirra no!*" he yelled.

The knife faltered.

From high above he heard a sound like tearing silk, and Echo came hurtling out of the sky, swung her talons, and struck the knife from Pirra's hand.

At the same moment, Hylas heard the spear hissing toward him, and threw himself sideways. Again Kreon lunged, but this time the spear faltered and Kreon screamed, a horrible gurgling cry as the bull's horn pierced his back and burst through his breastplate. The great beast tossed him high. Still screaming and spraying blood, Kreon flew over its back in grisly imitation of a bull-leaper, and hit the stones with a crack. The bull swung around and gored him again, stabbing and trampling until all that remained was a bloody horror, and the son of Koronos had been obliterated by the savage guardian of the land he had dared to invade.

Shielding his eyes from the glare, Hylas watched the brightness leave the girl on the balcony. She was Pirra again, blinking and looking about as if she'd just woken up.

He saw the bull swing around with a snort and trot off, leaving the trampled remains in a spreading pool of blood.

Then, from the corner of his eye, Hylas glimpsed shadowy forms emerging from doorways in a seething black cloud of Plague. Silently, the ghosts converged on Kreon's corpse and dipped in their fingers and tasted his blood. Then a wind came whistling across the Great Court and blew away the Plague. Hylas sensed that the ghosts were no longer angry and lost, and with a sigh they too blew away, up to their long rest on the Ridge of the Dead.

Hylas thought of the ghostly children on the coast. Maybe they were no longer lost, and had found their dead parents; and maybe the other ghosts he'd seen on his wanderings were also finding peace in the tombs of their ancestors—for although the Sun hadn't returned and the Great Cloud hung as heavy as ever, the gods had blown away the Plague.

But now as he stood swaying on the stones, he sensed one last ghost moving toward him. She felt different from the others: a tall woman with long hair, who wasn't Keftian, but Akean—and she hadn't died of Plague. There was something incredibly familiar about her, something that pierced his heart with longing.

As she drew closer, Hylas shut his eyes and felt her palm

against his cheek, cool and light as a moth's wing. He heard her misty whisper in his ear. *Hylas . . . Your sister lives . . . Find her . . . Forgive me . . . Forgive your father . . . Forgive . . .*

With a cry, Hylas reached out to clutch his mother's hand, but his fingers grasped empty air. He ran after her, and she smiled at him over her shoulder; then a breeze came moaning over the stones and she faded to nothing before his eyes.

There was a lump in his chest. It hurt so much that he gasped and sank to his knees, fighting tears.

It took him a while to notice that the bull was trotting toward him. He saw its scarlet horns and the threatening tilt of its head; but he felt no fear, only a vast weariness.

The bull halted ten paces from him and pawed the stones.

"I c-can't fight you anymore," stammered Hylas.

As he knelt before the great beast, a golden blur darted between them—and there was Havoc, snarling at the bull.

Almost gratefully, the bull decided it had had enough, and swung around and plodded off, down the ramp and into the peaceful gloom of the understory. Then Havoc shook herself and bounded over to Hylas and gave his face a rasping lick.

He couldn't hold it back any longer. Flinging his arms around the lion cub's neck, he burst into painful, wrenching sobs for the mother he had never known, but who he now knew was dead and gone forever, and for the dream that he'd clung to all his life: That someday, he and Issi and their mother would all be together.

⸻

Pirra felt the wind in her face and saw the snakes drop from her arms and slither off to explore Kunisu.

She found that she was standing on the West Balcony, high above the Great Court. She felt empty and weak, with a pounding pain in her head. The sky was still ashen; the Sun had not returned. Dimly, Pirra remembered Echo striking the knife from her hand. The Goddess had sent Her creature to avert the sacrifice. But why? All Pirra knew was that Echo was perched on her shoulder, and she was alive, and so was Hylas.

He sat with his back against the sacred tree, with Havoc beside him and the double axe at his feet. His leather kilt was dusty, his bare chest scraped and bloodied. As she watched, the wind blew back his yellow hair, and for a moment he reminded her of the god of the hunt in the Hall of Whispers. Then it passed, and he was a boy again, staring fixedly ahead.

Some time later, Pirra found her way down to the Great Court. The smell of blood hung in the air, and she tried not to look at the horror on the stones.

Havoc watched Echo swoop down to perch in the sacred tree, but Hylas stared unseeingly ahead. As Pirra drew closer, she was startled to see that his cheeks were wet with tears.

Havoc came and rubbed against her thigh. The cub's

furry warmth made Pirra feel more and more herself. She had failed to complete the Mystery, but she had tried. Sadly, she wondered if her mother knew.

Hylas became aware of her, and sniffed and wiped his face on the back of his hand. His eyelashes were spiky, his tawny eyes glassy with tears.

Pushing Havoc gently away, Pirra knelt and put her hand on his shoulder and said his name.

## 35

She *sounded* like Pirra, but she had the eerily perfect face of the Goddess. Hylas was too dazed to take in what she was saying.

Now she was gripping his hand in hers and leading him along passages, with Havoc running behind.

"The Plague's gone," he mumbled. "The gods blew it away."

"But I couldn't complete the Mystery," she said. "I couldn't bring back the Sun."

After many twists and turns, they reached a shadowy space where she halted, staring at a smear of blood on the floor. "He's gone. Telamon's gone."

"*Telamon?*" cried Hylas.

"He fell. I thought he was dead, but he's gone."

With a jolt, Hylas' wits returned. "He could be any-where, and I've left my weapons in the Great Court, we've got to get out of here!"

"That's what I've been *saying*!" said Pirra.

Back in her room, Hylas ignored the chaos of trampled food and well-chewed sheepskins and started gathering their gear, while Pirra hurriedly flung on her own clothes and washed her face, completing the change from goddess to girl.

"You knew Telamon once," she said, cramming her things in a calfskin bag. "What will he do now?"

"He won't leave Kreon's body behind, his clan worships their ancestors. When he's dealt with that, he'll come after us, no matter how badly he's hurt."

She paused. "He thinks I have the dagger."

The dagger. Hylas had forgotten it, but now his thoughts flew to Userref. Keftiu was vast. How would they ever find him?

The wind was getting up, moaning over the roofs and howling through passages. Suddenly, a savage gust blew aside the door-hanging. Pirra's eyes widened. "It sounds angry."

Hylas slung his cloak about him and shouldered his gear. "Come on. Dusk soon, and there's a storm on the way."

A gust of wind shook the tent, and the slave bandaging Telamon's head cringed.

"Storm on the way," said Ilarkos.

Telamon gave him a cold stare. "So let me be clear. We sent you up that mountain with half our men to catch whoever was up there—and you failed."

"They slipped away in the dark—"

"Why didn't you come and help us in the House of the Goddess?"

"We've only just made it back to camp!"

"Excuses!" Telamon barked at the slave, who refilled his wine cup.

Haggard with fatigue, Ilarkos watched thirstily. "We saw peasants on the move, my lord. They're returning to their villages, the priests say the Plague's gone. Among them I saw that Egyptian who was her slave. His face was dead white, it was horrible, like a ghost—"

"Ghosts!" sneered Telamon. He drained his cup. Maybe wine would ease the pain in his head.

He had a hazy memory of coming to his senses in a dark corner of that dreadful place and staggering around seeking a way out, then finding himself at a window on an upper story overlooking a vast open court. He'd seen Pirra on a balcony, her white arms raised like a goddess; a bull trampling Kreon's corpse; and a *lion* leaping to Hylas' defense.

Telamon ground his teeth. Lions were for *chieftains,* not goatherds; there were lions painted above the gates of his grandfather's citadel at Mycenae. It's all wrong, he thought savagely. Why Hylas and not me?

The wind roared in the pines and shook the tent. His men were huddled around their fires, shocked by their leader's ghastly death. He should go and rally them, but he felt too angry and bitter to try.

"My lord," said Ilarkos, "what are your orders? Do we return to Mycenae? These Keftians are no fighters, but if they turn on us, we'll be hopelessly outnumbered."

Telamon went still. For the first time, Ilarkos had asked *him* for orders. His anger vanished. Everything made sense. He had prayed for a chance to prove himself leader, and the gods had heard him. *They had killed Kreon—so that he, Telamon, might lead.* He would find the dagger and restore it to Mycenae. It was his destiny.

And maybe Pirra had told the truth when she said she didn't have the dagger. Maybe she'd sent it away.

Flinging aside his cup, Telamon rose. "We will set sail for Mycenae, but not yet."

"My lord?"

"At first light, the men will retrieve my uncle's remains and burn them with all honor, as befits a son of Koronos. Then we go after the Egyptian. That was no ghost you saw. He's alive and he has the dagger, or he knows where she hid it. Either way, we don't leave Keftiu without him."

———

Userref had shaved off his eyebrows in mourning and whitened his face with lime. Now, as lightning flared and rain hammered down, he kneeled on the windswept hillside and shouted prayers to his gods. "Auset, Protectress of the Dead, watch over she whom I loved as a little sister! Heru, Lord of Light, transform her spirit into a falcon, for her heart is righteous in the great balance!"

But he knew it was hopeless. Why should the gods of Egypt hear him, when Pirra had been a barbarian?

Someone grabbed him by the shoulders and hauled him

to his feet. "What are you *doing*?" yelled a voice in Akean. "Don't you know the Crows are after you?"

The stranger was strong, dragging Userref downhill and deep into the woods, where he found an abandoned farmhouse hidden in a thicket, kicked open the door, flung Userref inside, and slammed it shut behind him. "What were you *doing*? D'you *want* them to kill you?"

Userref backed away, clutching his precious bundle. "If they did, I'd deserve it for letting her die!"

The stranger snorted. "Then why'd you paint crows on the soles of your boots? I thought Egyptians did that to curse their enemies!"

Userref was startled. Who was this man, that he knew the ways of Egypt?

The stranger was tall and broad-shouldered, with the long dark hair and uncouth beard of an Akean. He looked poor, but the fierce intelligence in his light-gray eyes warned Userref that he was no ordinary wanderer.

Alarmed, he watched the stranger pull a wineskin from the sack on his shoulder and cut a hunk of grimy cheese with a large bronze knife. "So why are they after you?" he said with his mouth full.

"My mistress fell ill," Userref said guardedly. "I went to fetch dittany. When I returned, I found a smoking ruin. Later I saw their leader with her sealstone on his wrist . . ." He choked. "She died by *fire*, so her spirit is incomplete and she can never gain eternal life!"

Thunder shook the farmhouse, and both men ducked.

"But Keftians have their own gods to look after their souls," said the stranger.

Userref wished he could believe that. But if only Egyptians knew how to attain eternal life, didn't that condemn *all* barbarians to oblivion? All he knew was that his little sister was dead, and he would never see her again.

"You still haven't told me why the Crows are after you," said the stranger.

"You're right, I haven't," Userref said politely. Slipping his hand inside his sack, he touched the snakeskin bundle that hid the dagger of Koronos. "Why did you help me?"

The Akean shrugged. "The Crows are my enemies. I saw them hunting you. And maybe—because you're a long way from home, and so am I . . . You must miss the land of the Great River," he added in Egyptian.

Userref's eyes stung. It was years since he'd heard it spoken by anyone but Pirra.

Then he had an alarming thought. Why would some ragged Akean cross his path, speaking Egyptian? *Was this man a god in disguise?* "Wh-who *are* you?" he faltered. "What do you seek?"

"Well, I wasn't seeking you. Let's just say I'm looking for some people I used to know who hate the Crows as much as I do. What about you? Where are you heading?"

Userref hesitated. He'd sworn to Pirra that he would keep the dagger safe until he found a way for a god to destroy it. But how *could* he, when he was an Egyptian, to whom the gods of Keftiu wouldn't listen?

If this man was a god, then *he* could destroy the dagger. But if he wasn't? The risk was too great. "I don't know," he said. "Where do you think I should go?"

The stranger who might be a god took a pull at the wineskin. "Go home."

Userref stared at him. "I can't."

"Why not? Your mistress is dead. Why stay on Keftiu?"

Hope leaped as Userref pictured the sacred papyrus waving on the banks of *Iteru*, and his long-lost family . . . And surely in Egypt he would find a way to honor Pirra's last wish.

Again, the stranger spoke in Egyptian. "Whatever you decide, my friend, may you have long life and the sight of the Sun, and find your way to eternal peace on the horizon."

Userref bowed low, in case this man really was a god, then returned the traditional blessing: "And may your name live forever in eternity. I shall do as you say."

# 36

Clutching her sodden cloak about her face to hide her scar, Pirra hurried after Hylas, who'd gone ahead to find Havoc. For two days they'd been desperately seeking Userref while the storm continued to rage—but still no sign of him.

Rounding a bend, she found Hylas confronting a gang of fishermen with three-pronged spears and weird purple skin. A flock of soggy sheep huddled in a pen adjoining a tumbledown farmhouse, and trapped between that and the pen was Havoc: wet, snarling, and terrified.

"Leave her alone!" shouted Hylas, grabbing one of the spear shafts.

"Don't you dare hurt her!" screamed Pirra.

"That thing's after our sheep!" yelled a fisherman.

Everyone shouted at once. Havoc seized her chance and shot off into the woods. "What's going on?" bellowed a voice.

At the door of the farmhouse Pirra saw a mountainous old woman swathed in what seemed to be a wet leather tent. She had a face like a purple sponge and only one eye, which lurched from Pirra to Hylas—and glared at him. "*You!*" she rasped.

---

"Who's she?" said Gorgo, jerking her head at Pirra.

"Just some girl," said Hylas.

Gorgo snorted, and he sensed that she saw through Pirra's disguise, but didn't care.

They were all in the farmhouse, including Gorgo's elderly dog and the sheep, and her sons were busy ransacking the place. The air was a fug of wet livestock and dye-workers' stink of urine and rotting fish.

"Do you *know* this woman?" whispered Pirra beside him.

"I met her when I first got to Keftiu," he hissed.

"Is this their farm?"

"No, but I wouldn't point that out!" Then to Gorgo, "Are we prisoners?"

Gorgo ignored that. "A few nights ago," she said accusingly, "we hear of Crows on Setoya. Then this storm washes away the Plague, so we come to see what we can find. Suddenly there's a *lion* attacking our sheep—and now you! *You* tell *me* what's going on!"

"We're hiding from the Crows," said Hylas, "and we're looking for—"

"Crows are gone," snapped Gorgo. "Man called Deukaryo ganged up with a whole crowd of farmers, forced them at spear point onto a fishing boat." Her laugh shook her vast bulk. "Some lad on board with a bandaged head yelling about the Angry Ones. They'll not be back to Keftiu in a hurry."

A dreadful thought occurred to Hylas. Maybe the Crows had found Userref; maybe Telamon had the dagger.

Pirra had thought of that too. "You've got to let us go!" she cried. "We're looking for an Egyptian, we have to find him! Did the Crows catch him?"

Thunder shook the farmhouse. "You're not going anywhere in this," growled Gorgo.

—◦◦◦—

Pirra was curled up asleep and Gorgo sat snoring by the fire with her dog at her feet. Hylas listened to the creak of the rafters and wondered if the same storm was battering Messenia—and if Issi was sheltering somewhere, thinking of her brother.

Ever since Kunisu, his mother's death had weighed on his heart like a stone. He knew Pirra was wondering what was wrong, but he couldn't bring himself to tell her.

And he was worried about Havoc. Whether or not they found Userref, they couldn't stay on Keftiu, or someone would recognize Pirra and drag her back to Kunisu; but what about Havoc?

He was roused by the smell of singed fur: The dog's rump was beginning to scorch. Quietly, Hylas shifted its bottom, and it thumped its tail in its sleep.

"You're a long way from Mount Lykas, aren't you, lad?" rasped Gorgo.

He met her cloudy eye. "I never told you I was from there."

"You didn't need to. I knew your mother."

He went still. "My mother's dead. Her ghost came to me in the Great Court at Kunisu. How did you know her?"

She spat a gob of purple snot. "She was a Marsh Dweller; an Outsider of the coast. They got on well with us Messenians. I was older than her, but we were friends." She gave a rumbling laugh. "We both fell for handsome foreigners. I fetched up here. She went north to the mountains near Mycenae—"

"*Mycenae?*" said Hylas.

"He was Mountain Clan. But you must know that, you've got his tattoo."

Hylas stared at the mark on his forearm. "But—this is a Crow tattoo. They did it when I was a slave, I turned it into a bow by scratching a line along the bottom."

"Well, it's the mark of the Mountain Clan. You're the image of your father." With a blotchy purple paw, she scratched her chins. "They quarreled. Your mother knew the Crows would invade, but he didn't believe it, so she took you and Issi and went south."

"You—you know my sister's name."

Gorgo shrugged. "Means *frog* in your mother's tongue. She liked frogs."

Hylas was reeling. His father had been Mountain Clan, the clan that had refused to fight the Crows. His father had been a coward.

"She never got as far as Messenia," muttered Gorgo. "You were too small."

"So she left us on Mount Lykas," said Hylas in a low voice. "Wrapped in a bearskin."

"Bears," grunted Gorgo. "Sacred to your father's clan. She left you and went to fetch help."

With a stick, Hylas jabbed at the fire. "Why didn't she come back?"

"She got sick and died," Gorgo said brutally. "By the time her father heard about you, some peasant had taken you to his village."

Her father . . . Hylas remembered the scrawny old Outsider who used to teach him the ways of the wild. "He was my grandfather. He never told us, why didn't he *tell* us?"

"Who knows? I heard all this long after, when someone from my village turned up here. Maybe the old man couldn't bear to talk about her, maybe he blamed your father for her death—"

"He was right about that, wasn't he?" Hylas burst out. "If it hadn't been for my father, she wouldn't have died and we wouldn't have spent years slaving for some lousy old peasant!"

"Well, it's *done*," snapped Gorgo. "You're not the first boy to lose his parents."

⸺

Shortly before dawn, Hylas shook Pirra awake. "Come on," he muttered. "Dawn soon, we're free to go."

"Didn't you sleep?" yawned Pirra.

"No," he said curtly.

Outside it was still dark and as stormy as ever. As they

headed off beneath the dripping trees, Gorgo appeared in the doorway and called to him.

"Watch yourself on the road, lad! Odd people about. My sons saw a weird one a while back. Face smeared with lime, said he was in mourning. Could've been a madman—or an Egyptian."

"Where was he heading?" cried Pirra.

Gorgo jerked her head. "Turonija. East along the coast."

# 37

Pirra asked Hylas if he was all right.

"Well, let's see," he said, raising his voice above the storm. "We can't find Userref; sooner or later someone's going to recognize you and drag you back to Kunisu; and we can't find Havoc either, so she probably thinks I've abandoned her."

Pirra pushed her wet hair out of her face. "She might just be lost, but she'll find us."

"Mm," he said gloomily.

Hoisting her bag on her shoulder, Pirra started up the hill. "We might be able to see her from the top."

Instead of following her, Hylas grabbed a stick and decapitated a bush. He *wanted* to tell her about his parents, but he couldn't. Anger and shame churned inside him. He was the son of a coward who'd fled the Crows rather than fight.

"Wait for me!" he shouted after Pirra. But the wind was too loud and she didn't hear.

---

Miserably, the cub plodded through the thorn bushes. She couldn't find the boy, and it was frightening being alone in the storm. Trees flung branches at her, and she was nearly squashed by a falling pine. When she emerged from the bushes, her fur was all snarly with thorns. Wearily, she sat down to lick them off.

From high above came the falcon's shivering cry.

The cub stopped licking. The falcon was calling to the girl. And wherever the girl was, the boy wouldn't be far— so they were *bound* to find each other eventually.

Feeling better, the lion cub headed off, keeping the falcon in view.

And of course, the boy would be looking for her too. The cub was as sure of this as she was of the spots on her paws: He would never abandon her again.

———

The falcon *still* hadn't made her first kill. Bats, crows, magpies, they'd all escaped; it was *so* humiliating.

The Wind was lumpy and kept trying to fling her off, but at last she found an updraft, and below her the girl and the poor plodding lion cub dwindled to specks.

That cub. Why did she like it so much when the boy scratched her flanks? The thought of anyone scratching the falcon's feathers made her feel sick.

And yet. She couldn't help admiring the cub's stubborn determination to find the boy. It made the falcon feel that if she also kept trying, she might make her first kill.

Far below, she spotted a flock of birds, so she tilted one wing and slid across the sky to take a look. Pigeons. Flying upwind.

Again the falcon caught the updraft, this time soaring so high that she burst through the clouds into a dazzling glare. For the first time ever, she was face-to-face with the vast power she'd always sensed hidden beyond the clouds. She knew at once that this was the Sun.

Still she climbed, until the height made her ears sing. She would fly higher than she'd ever flown before.

And then she would dive.

On the hilltop, Pirra slitted her eyes against the rain. Below her the dirty Sea crashed on the shore, and a group of peasants straggled homeward. The storm was still punishing Keftiu and the Sun was never coming back. She had failed Keftiu and she'd failed her mother. And Userref had vanished without a trace.

Glancing skyward, she glimpsed a dark speck against the gray. It was Echo. Pirra's spirits lifted a little.

A flock of pigeons sped past. Echo was going after them. As Pirra watched, she felt that she too was hunting, experiencing the rush of limitless flight . . .

She is Echo. The earth falls away as she spirals higher and gets ready to dive. Now she's tucking her legs beneath her tail and folding her wings, she's hurtling toward the prey.

Faster than an arrow she plummets through the screaming air: faster than any creature who's ever lived. Her eyes lock on to a pigeon that's strayed from the rest. The pigeon swerves. She adjusts her dive to follow. As she hurtles closer, she swings her legs forward and clenches her talons—she punches into the pigeon, snapping its spine and knocking it out of the sky.

With a jolt, Pirra was herself again. "You did it!" she yelled, jumping up and down.

Echo caught the prey in one talon before it hit the ground and flew to a branch, where she ripped off its head and started plucking feathers from its breast.

"You did it," murmured Pirra. She was breathless and exhilarated, as if she too had flown faster than thought.

It was then she became aware that the rain had stopped. The wind had sunk to a gentle breeze. The thornscrub was no longer grimy with ash; the storm had washed it clean. She was *hot*.

Below her Hylas was trudging uphill. Suddenly, a yellow blur burst from the bushes and streaked toward him. "Havoc!" he cried. Then the lion cub knocked him over and they were rolling together in the rain-washed thyme.

Pirra caught her breath. Hylas' hair was shining like gold. Then the gods tore away the last of the Great Cloud that had blighted Keftiu for so long, and she turned up her face to a sky of astonishing blue—and shielded her eyes from the life-giving glare of the eternal Sun.

⸺◦⸺

"You did it," said Hylas.

"But I didn't complete the Mystery," said Pirra.

"No, but that's because the Goddess sent Echo to save

you. Maybe—maybe the Goddess decided that you'd done enough."

Pirra didn't reply. They stood watching the peasants on the shore falling to their knees and stretching out their arms to the Sun.

Havoc, washed a clean glossy gold, rubbed her forehead against Hylas' thigh, and he scratched her ears. Then she turned her head, and her tawny eyes caught something far to the west. Following her gaze, he made out the white shimmer of Kunisu. He felt a twinge in his temple, and glimpsed a tall gray figure on the Ridge of the Dead.

"I wonder if she knows," Pirra said shakily.

Hylas saw the ghost of Yassassara nod once, then fade back into her tomb. "She knows," he said.

---

By the time they reached Turonija, spring had arrived in a rush. Almond and olive trees burst into flower. Green spears of barley shot up, and flaxfields became drifts of brilliant blue. Hills throbbed with scarlet poppies, yellow broom, and white asphodel, and the wind was warm and fragrant with hyacinth. Crickets rasped, frogs piped—while in the Sea, shoals of tiny silver fish darted about, cleaning up the shallows. All Keftiu was on the move: washing, rebuilding, burying.

"I'm glad you're seeing it at its best," said Pirra.

Hylas glanced at her. "Will you be sorry to leave?"

"No. Yes. I don't know." She gave a crooked smile. Once they left Keftiu, she could never return. If the priests caught her, they would drag her back to Kunisu and keep her there, or sell her off in marriage to some chieftain far across the Sea. Daughters of High Priestesses were not allowed to be free.

But now that the Sun had returned, Hylas felt more hopeful. Pirra had told him that she'd overheard his talk with Gorgo, and that was a huge relief, as it meant he didn't have to talk about his mother. And to Pirra's lasting joy, although Echo was now hunting for herself, she seemed keen to stay close.

And yet they still hadn't found Userref.

Turonija was a big settlement that had been wrecked by the Great Wave, but was now a hive of activity: men rebuilding houses, women making offerings and cooking pots. Twice, Pirra hid her scar and went to seek news of Userref, but no one had heard of a wandering Egyptian. What she did learn was that the priests were preparing to choose a new High Priestess, and in Kunisu they'd found the remains of a Mystery; word had spread like wildfire that Yassassara's daughter had brought back the Sun— then turned into a falcon and flown away.

"I'm glad they know it was you," said Hylas. "And it's good that they think you're gone. Now they won't be looking for you."

Pirra didn't reply.

They were on a hill feathered with tamarisk trees, looking west toward Kunisu. As they watched, the sky was briefly dimmed by cloudshadow; then the Sun blazed out, and the House of the Goddess glittered like crystal.

"That's how I want to remember it," said Pirra. Her face was taut, her fists clenched at her sides. Hylas put his arm around her, and for a moment she leaned against him. Then she ran off, calling for Echo.

Just beyond Turonija, they found a secluded cove, where they agreed that Hylas would wait with Havoc, while Pirra slipped back and tried yet again to learn something of Userref.

Havoc was scared of the Sea, so to put her at her ease, Hylas crouched down and let the waves lap his feet. The cub edged forward and pawed the water—but fled when it came surging in. Then Echo swooped, her wingtips skimming the waves, and this seemed to give Havoc courage. Soon she was happily splashing about, and Hylas was trailing seaweed for her to hunt.

Pirra came back at a run, looking fraught. "He's gone!" she panted.

"What? Where?"

She met his eyes. "Egypt."

"*Egypt?*" He was appalled. "Are you sure?"

"He bought passage on a ship a few days ago."

"But—Egypt! That's at the end of the world."

"I should have realized. He thinks I'm dead, and I made him swear to keep it safe . . ."

Hylas stared out to Sea. "I suppose—he will try to destroy it?"

"Yes, but he's Egyptian; his way of doing that will be

simply to wait and let things take their course!"

He nodded. "And it's only a matter of time before the Crows find out where it is, and go after him."

"We can't risk it. So I suppose—this means we go to Egypt."

Hylas didn't reply. However hard he tried to get back to Akea and find Issi, the gods always sent him farther away. First the Island of the Fin People, then Thalakrea, then Keftiu, and now—"*Egypt*," he said out loud. "How are we ever going to get there?"

Pirra gave him a strange look. "Well, at least buying our passage isn't going to be hard." Taking her bag from her shoulder, she tipped a clinking river of jewels onto the seaweed.

Hylas stared at great golden collars hung with flashing scarlet and leaf-green stones, silver anklets and long ropes of amethyst and lapis lazuli.

Pirra was trying not to look smug.

"You brought these from Kunisu," he said in disbelief.

She broke into a smile. "Of course I did. You're always telling me the first rule of survival is to sort your day's food and water. I just went a bit further."

Hylas scratched his head. Then he snorted a laugh. "I can't believe I didn't think of that."

"I can't believe you didn't either," said Pirra, elbowing him in the ribs.

He elbowed her back, and with a yelp she fell over, then chucked a handful of seaweed at him. Soon they were staggering about, pelting each other. Havoc bounded up from the Sea to join in, and shook herself, soaking them both.

"Although there is one problem," said Pirra a bit later as she was brushing herself off.

"What's that?" said Hylas, pushing Havoc's cold wet muzzle out of his face.

"How are we going to get Havoc on a ship?"

Hylas blinked.

The lion cub glanced from him to Pirra, as if she knew they were talking about her.

"She hated the voyage to Keftiu," said Pirra, "she was seasick the whole journey."

Hylas looked at Havoc; then at Echo, soaring overhead, and finally at Pirra—and his spirits lifted. He felt that as long as they all stayed together, he could do anything and journey anywhere, yes, even to Egypt.

Stooping for a pebble, he sent it skimming across the waves. Then he smiled at Pirra. "We'll find a way," he said.

# Author's Note

*The Eye of the Falcon* takes place three and a half thousand years ago in the Bronze Age, in what we call ancient Greece. But this was long before the time of marble temples with which you may be familiar. It was even before the Greeks ranged their gods into an orderly pantheon of Zeus, Hera, Hades, and others.

We don't know as much about Bronze Age Greece, because its people left so few written records, but we know something about their astonishing cultures, which we call the Mycenaeans and the Minoans. Theirs is the world of Gods and Warriors. It's thought that this was a world of scattered chieftaincies, separated by mountain ranges and forests, and that it was wetter and greener than today, with far more wild animals in both land and sea.

To create the world of Hylas and Pirra, I've studied the archaeology of the Greek Bronze Age. To get an idea of people's thoughts and beliefs, I've drawn on those of more recent peoples who still live in traditional ways, as I did in my Stone Age series, Chronicles of Ancient Darkness. And although people in Hylas' time lived mostly by farming or fishing, I've no doubt that much of the knowledge and beliefs of the Stone Age hunter-gatherers lived on into the Bronze Age, particularly among the poorer people, such as Hylas himself.

A quick word about place-names: Akea (or Achaea, as it's often spelled) is the ancient name for mainland Greece; Lykonia is my name for present-day Lakonia. I've kept the name Mycenae unchanged, as it's so well-known, and adopted the name "Keftian" for the great Cretan civilization we call Minoan. (We don't know what they called themselves; depending on which book you read, their name may have been Keftians, or that may just have been a name given them by the ancient Egyptians.) As for Egypt, although that name derives from the Greeks, I've kept it because, like Mycenae, it felt too artificial to change.

The map of the World of Gods and Warriors shows the world as Hylas and Pirra experience it, so it leaves out some islands that aren't part of the story, and includes others which I've made up, such as the Island of the Fin People, and Thalakrea. The same goes for the map of Keftiu: I've included only those places important to the story, such as Taka Zimi (which I've moved from the site of its real counterpart). In reality, Minoan Crete had many more settlements, palaces, and so on than I've shown, but I've left these out, as they would have cluttered up the map.

To create Keftiu as Hylas and Pirra know it, I've been to Crete several times and explored many Minoan sites, including Knossos, Phaestos, Gournia, Petras, Zakros and the cave at Psyhro. I climbed to the incredibly windy peak sanctuary at Juktas, which gave me ideas for Setoya. I found my way through the Gorge of the Dead at the extreme east of the island. The fact that its caves contain unexcavated tombs gives it a rather spooky feel, and on the day I walked the length of the gorge, the only other creatures I saw (apart from goats) was a pair of peregrine falcons having a noisy spat with a couple of ravens.

To get ideas for Taka Zimi, I visited the ruined sanctuary at Kato Syme on the flanks of Mount Dikte. Even today it's hard to find, and feels astonishingly remote. I was there on a misty, overcast day with clouds seeping over the crags. It was easy to imagine Pirra's feelings on being imprisoned there.

The House of the Goddess, or Kunisu, is *based* on Knossos, the greatest of the Minoan "palaces" (that's what we call them today, although we're not sure how they were used)—but I need to make clear that I've changed it to suit the story. The layout is different and so are the rooms. Also, I've added details from other Minoan ruins; for example, the loo comes from one in Akrotiri on present-day Santorini (which I also visited). I've visited the real Knossos several times, and my most useful visit by far was when Professor Todd Whitelaw kindly took time out from field-work at Knossos to show me over the site, including the Little Palace and the Unexplored Mansion, and let me examine some of his recent finds. One of the many valuable insights I gained was that the hills surrounding the site are riddled with as yet unexcavated tombs. This gave me a powerful sense of how Pirra feels at the thought of her mother looking down at her from the Ridge of the Dead.

Many of the features which Hylas and Pirra encounter inside Kunisu, such as the wall paintings, the sacrificial vessel shaped like a bull's head, and the ivory god, are based on real Minoan artefacts I've seen in the museums at Heraklion, Athens, and Archanes, and others. The ivory god was inspired by the "Palaikastro Kouros" in the Archaeological Museum in Sitia. This figure was made of gold, rock crystal, serpentine, and hippopotamus ivory. It was smashed and burned three and a half thousand years ago, but even in his damaged form, he remains an astonishing masterpiece of Minoan sculpture.

To get a feel for how Havoc experiences life, I've spent time with four Asiatic lion cubs at Paignton Zoo, where Senior Keeper Helen Neighbour kindly let me get as close to them as even she could get, given the presence of their enormous and very watchful mother; she also answered my myriad questions about their habits and characters. To gain insights into how Echo perceives the world, I've visited several falconries and watched countless displays, as well as spending time with peregrine falcons and their falconers at close quarters, to understand the birds' habits and characteristics. Needless to say, the way Pirra brings up Echo is a bit different from the ways of western falconry as practiced today. I've incorporated methods from

## Author's Note

falconry as practiced in different parts of the world, and also simplified things a bit, to suit the needs of the story.

I want to thank the many people (too numerous to name) who gave me advice and assistance while I was in Crete and Santorini, and in particular, Irini Kouraki and Manolis Melissourgakis, who were my guide and driver respectively in Crete, and without whose local knowledge and kindness I would never have found Kato Syme. I also want to thank Sarah Hesford at the English School of Falconry for letting me get near some fascinating peregrine falcons and for answering my many questions; and Helen Neighbour, Senior Keeper at Paignton Zoo, for giving so generously of her time and letting me get so close to those gorgeous lion cubs. I'm also extremely grateful, as always, to Todd Whitelaw, Professor of Aegean Archaeology at the Institute of Archaeology, University College London, for showing me over Knossos and answering my endless questions on the prehistoric Aegean, as well as providing invaluable guidance on the various Cretan sites I visited alone, and the significance of what I might see there.

Finally, and as always, I want to thank my wonderful agent Peter Cox for his indefatigable commitment and support, and my hugely talented editor at Puffin Books, Ben Horslen, for his lively and imaginative response to the story of Hylas and Pirra.

*Michelle Paver, 2014*

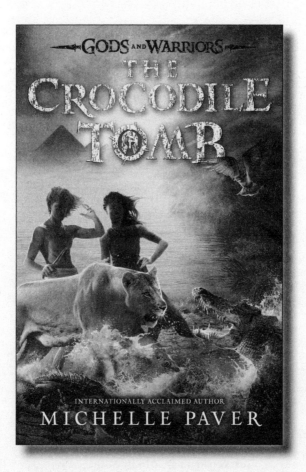

I

"This is like no land I've ever seen," muttered Hylas. "There's nothing here." Only the Sea lying stunned beneath the Sun, and this vast shimmering plain of endless red sand.

"It's nothing like Egypt, either," said Pirra. "Userref said Egypt's got a huge river down the middle, and fields and villages and temples along the banks. He said . . ." She licked her lips. "He said that on either side of it there's only endless red sand. He called it—*deshret*."

"Desert," said Hylas.

She met his eyes. "It's where they bury their dead."

*Deshret.*

The Sun was fiercer than he'd ever known, the air so hot it was like breathing smoke. Squinting in the glare, he scanned the quivering plain. No villages, no river. Just the odd clump of rocks and dusty scrub, and a twist of wind-blown sand whirling like a demon over the ground.

Far out on the Sea, their ship had dwindled to a speck. "They never intended to take us to Egypt," he said bitterly. "They stole our gold and dumped us here to die."

"They could've killed us and chucked us overboard," Pirra pointed out. "And they did leave us our weapons."

"What, so we're *lucky*?"

"No, but we're alive."

She was right—but he wanted to rage and fling curses at those filthy, lying Phoenicians. For over a moon, he and Pirra had hidden in the Keftian hills with Echo and Havoc, desperately waiting for a ship bound for Egypt. When at last they'd found one willing to take them, it had been blown off course, and the crew had blamed *them*. "Foreigners bring bad luck," the captain had declared. And who could be more outlandish than an Akean boy with strange tawny hair and a young lioness at his side, and a Keftian girl with a crescent-moon scar on her cheek and a falcon on her wrist?

Havoc padded past Hylas, then glanced back at him for reassurance. She still behaved like a cub, as if she hadn't yet realized that she was nearly full-grown. After days of sea sickness, she was gaunt and bedraggled, and now besieged by flies. She stood panting, miserably twitching her ears.

Hylas untied the neck of the waterskin and poured a little into his cupped hand; and she slurped it up with a rasping lick that nearly took the skin off his palm. "Sorry I can't give you more," he told her. The waterskin was only half full. It wouldn't last long.

"Maybe Egypt's not far away," said Pirra. "Rivers flow into the Sea, don't they? If we walk along the coast, we might find it."

"Unless we go the wrong way and end up heading deeper into the desert."

Echo, soaring overhead, suddenly wheeled off across the plain. "Maybe she knows where it is," said Pirra, watching the falcon fly.

Hylas didn't reply. Echo could fly for days without water. They couldn't. He could see Pirra thinking the same thing. "Come on," he said. "Let's dig a hole, see if we can find anything to drink."

A searing wind flung grit in his eyes as they trudged up the shore. Sweat trickled down his back, soaking the coil of rope slung across his shoulder. He felt the ground burning through the soles of his rawhide sandals. Around him the heat danced, so that his shadow seemed to be moving on its own. There was a throbbing pain in his skull. He prayed that was only the glare, and not the ache he always got before a vision.

Fifty paces in from the Sea, they knelt and started digging with their hands. They dug as far as they could. Soon, moisture seeped into the bottom of the hole. Hylas tasted it—and spat it out. "Salt," he said in disgust.

Pirra cast about her. "Berries on that bush over there. Can we eat them?"

Hylas blinked. He was an Outsider who'd grown up in the wild; he knew every plant in Akea. But he'd never seen this one. "I don't know," he said uneasily. "We can't risk it, it might be poisonous."

Havoc padded over to the bush and slumped down in its

pitiful strip of shade, batting at the flies with her forepaws.

The bush gave an angry hiss.

Havoc scrambled to her feet and backed away.

Before Hylas or Pirra could take in what was happening, a snake shot out from under the bush. But instead of slithering off, it turned and rose up on the end of its tail—it swayed its flat black head from side to side, and *spat* at Havoc. She dodged. The jet of venom missed her eye and hit her nose instead. Hylas threw his knife. It struck just behind the head, pinning the snake to the sand. As it twisted and thrashed, Pirra finished it off with a rock.

A shaken silence.

Havoc sneezed and rubbed her muzzle in the sand. Hylas retrieved his knife and hacked off the snake's head.

"Have you ever seen a snake do that?" panted Pirra.

"No," he said curtly.

They exchanged glances. Killing the first creature they met had to be a bad omen. And for all they knew, this snake was sacred to whatever strange gods ruled this land.

Havoc was patting the carcass with a curious forepaw. Hylas pushed her aside and wiped the last of the venom off her nose with the hem of his tunic.

"D'you think we can eat it?" said Pirra.

"I don't know," he muttered. Anger tightened his throat. "I don't *know*!" he cried, lashing out at the bush with his knife. "I don't *know* these plants or these creatures! I don't *know* if we can eat these berries, and I've never seen a snake stand on its tail and spit!"

"Hylas, stop it, you're frightening Havoc!"

The young lioness had retreated behind Pirra's legs, and was staring at him with her ears back.

"Sorry," he mumbled.

Havoc came over and rubbed her furry cheek against his thigh. He scratched her big golden head, as much to reassure himself as her.

"When I first met you," Pirra said levelly, "we were stuck on an island with no food and no water. But we survived."

"That was different."

"I know, but if anyone can survive out here, it's you."

Echo swept down onto Pirra's shoulder and gave a lock of her dark hair an affectionate tug. Pirra touched the falcon's scaly yellow foot with one finger.

Havoc was gazing up at him, her great golden eyes full of trust.

"Right," he said. "We've got half a skin of water, two knives, my slingshot, a coil of rope, and a dead snake. *If* we can eat it."

"Animals know if something's poisoned, don't they?" said Pirra. "If Havoc and Echo think it's all right . . ."

Hylas nodded. "Let's find out." Cutting a chunk off the tail, he tossed it to Havoc, then gave a smaller piece to Pirra, who held it in her fist. Echo hopped onto the raw-hide cuff Pirra wore on her forearm, ripped the meat to shreds, and gulped it down. Havoc was already crunching hers messily to bits.

"Looks like it's all right," said Pirra.

"And there might be fish in the Sea," said Hylas.

She gave him a wry smile. "And the Phoenicians didn't get *all* the gold. I hid a necklace under my tunic—so if we can find someone selling food, we'll be fine!"

He snorted a laugh.

It was nearly noon. The heat was unbearable.

"Havoc had the right idea," he said. "We've got to get out of this sun."

Pirra pointed up the coast, where a rocky outcrop shimmered in the distance. "Might be a cave among those rocks."

"Let's go."

Hylas felt a bit better. But as they started toward the rocks, he realized that finding Egypt, and Userref, and the dagger of Koronos, no longer mattered.

First, they had to stay alive.

## 2

They'd cut strips off their tunics and wet them in the Sea, then wound them around their heads. The sopping cloth had been wonderfully cool, but it soon dried, and now Pirra could feel the Sun hammering her skull. Her eyes were scratchy, her tongue was a lump of sand. She thought she kept hearing the trickle of water, but there wasn't any. Only the deathlike silence of the desert.

Hylas stumbled along beside her, squinting and rubbing his temples. She worried that he might be about to have a vision. What would he see? Ghosts? Demons? If it happened, he would tell her when he was ready, but she'd learned not to ask. He hated talking about it. "It's frightening and it hurts," he'd said once. "I never know when it's going to happen. I just wish it would stop."

The outcrop of big red boulders wasn't getting any closer. She wondered if it was really there, or just a trick of the gods.

A trick of the gods . . .

She halted. "Hylas, we're doing this all wrong."

"What?" he croaked.

"Whatever gods rule this place, they won't help us till we've made an offering."

Hylas looked at her, appalled. "I can't believe I forgot."

"Me too. We should've done it as soon as we got ashore. We won't make it if we don't."

Hylas wiped the sweat off his face and tossed her the lion claw he wore on a thong around his neck, while she took off Userref's *wedjat* eye amulet, which she'd worn ever since Keftiu. Muttering a swift prayer under her breath, she found a clump of scrub and tucked the snake's head in its branches. It would be safe from Echo, who'd flown off to hunt; and Havoc was plodding ahead and hadn't noticed. After touching both amulets to the offering, Pirra stumbled back to Hylas and handed him his lion claw.

"Who did you offer to?" he said as they resumed their trudge.

"The Goddess for me, Lady of the Wild Things for you, and two of the most powerful gods of Egypt."

"Who?" He was scanning the ground for pebbles for his slingshot.

"*Heru*—He has a falcon's head—and *Sekhmet*, She has the head of a lioness. I remembered them because of Echo and Havoc."

Hylas slipped a pebble into the pouch at his belt. "Are there more?"

"Lots. Userref used to tell me stories when I was little . . ." She broke off. Userref had looked after her since she was a baby, and she missed him terribly. For fourteen years he'd played with her and scolded her, tried to keep her out of trouble, and told her all about his beloved Egypt. He was far more than a slave. He was the big brother she'd never had.

"Pirra?" said Hylas. "What are the other gods?"

"Um—there's one with the head of something called a jackal, I think that's a kind of fox. And one like a river horse—"

"A *what*?"

"They're very fat, with a huge snout, and they live in the river. Also there's a god like a crocodile, whatever that is."

He frowned. "When I was a slave down the mines, there was an Egyptian boy, he talked about crocodiles. He said they're giant lizards with hide tougher than armor, and they eat people. I thought he was making it up."

"I'm pretty sure they're real."

He didn't reply. He was squinting at the outcrop, which was now only forty paces away. "Your eyes are better than mine. Can you see people clambering about?"

Pirra's heart leaped. Through the shimmering air, she glimpsed tiny dark figures moving among the rocks. "The offering worked!" she croaked. "We're saved!"

⸺

The nearer they got, the more uneasy Hylas became. Those people moved astonishingly fast—but they were scrambling about on all fours.

He grabbed Pirra's arm. "Those aren't men!"

She shaded her eyes with her hand. "What *are* they?" she whispered.

They looked like a cross between men and dogs: covered in dense grayish brown fur; with thick tails; long, powerful arms; and narrow, bony red faces.

Hylas wondered if they were demons. But although he felt dizzy, and the rocks and even his shadow trembled in the heat, there was no burning finger stabbing his temple, as there always was when he had a vision.

Suddenly, he felt watched.

*"Look,"* breathed Pirra.

To their right, twenty paces from where they stood, one of the creatures crouched on top of a solitary boulder. It was bigger than the others; Hylas guessed it was the leader. He saw its massive chest matted with blood, its heavy brows overhanging small yellow eyes set very close together. Glaring at him.

"Don't run," Hylas said quietly. "Don't turn your back on it or it'll think we're prey."

Slowly, they began to edge backward.

The creature bared huge white fangs and uttered a harsh rattling bark. It sounded horribly like a signal.

Behind it, the other creatures had clustered at the base of the outcrop. They glanced up at their leader's barks, then went back to their kill. Hylas glimpsed the carcass of a large white buck with a long spiral horn. He saw strong man-like hands snapping its ribs, ripping open its belly, and clawing at glistening guts. One of the creatures grabbed the buck's hind leg and twisted it off as easily as if it had been a quail's wing.

On its boulder, the leader swung around, barking furiously. It wasn't barking at Hylas and Pirra.

Hylas' belly turned over.

Havoc was sneaking toward the carcass, intent on scaring away the creatures and seizing their prey, as she might scare away foxes or pine martens.

But these were no foxes.

"Havoc, come *back*!" shouted Hylas.

The young lioness knew her name well enough, but she ignored it. She hadn't been fed much on the ship, and a few chunks of snake weren't enough to blunt her hunger. The smell of fresh meat was agonizing.

"Havoc, come *back*!" yelled Hylas and Pirra together.

Havoc broke cover and charged, snarling and lashing out with her forepaws. But instead of scattering, the creatures raced *toward* her, barking furiously and gnashing their fangs. And now more of them were emerging from caves higher up, streaming down to join the attack, and the leader was hurtling over the sand at a dreadful shambling run.

Hylas and Pirra ran after him, Hylas yelling and firing pebbles with his slingshot, Pirra flinging whatever rocks she could find.

Havoc realized her mistake, turned tail, and fled. Hylas and Pirra did the same.

As he ran, Hylas glanced over his shoulder. The creatures weren't coming after them. They were leaping up and down at the foot of the outcrop, beating the ground with their fists.

Their leader sat on his haunches, glaring at the intruders who had dared approach his stronghold: *Stay away! Don't come back!*

---

"*Baboons*," panted Pirra some time later. "I knew Userref had mentioned them, I just couldn't remember the name."

"Is there a baboon god too?" gasped Hylas.

"I think so. They're incredibly clever and not afraid of anything."

"I could see that for myself!"

The Sun would be down soon, but the heat was still fierce. They had backtracked all the way down the shore, past where the Phoenicians had left them and where they'd killed the snake, and were now warily approaching another clump of boulders that looked as if it might provide shelter. If it wasn't full of baboons.

With his slingshot, Hylas pelted the outcrop with pebbles.

No angry barks, no vicious dog-men swarming out to attack.

Telling Pirra to wait, he climbed toward what appeared to be the mouth of a cave, flinging rocks as he went, to flush out anything hiding inside. A couple of bats flickered out of the darkness, but nothing else.

"It's clear," he called down. Dropping his gear, he

crawled inside. It was stifling, but any shade was a relief after the Sun.

Pirra crawled in too, and slumped onto her side. Her face was filmed with dust and sweat. When she peeled off her sandals, the thongs left her feet marked with red stripes.

The Sea wasn't far away, but they were too exhausted to stagger down and wash. What strength Hylas had left, he would need for setting snares.

He went outside again. From this vantage point, he saw a low rocky ridge not far off, and beyond it, the endless red desert, stretching to the end of the world.

The wind carried weird yelping calls. He wondered if they were jackals. He guessed that whatever creatures lived in the desert would hide from the Sun and come out at night. That was why Havoc, feeling the onset of dusk, had plodded off to hunt. Hylas only hoped she had the sense to stalk lizards or hares—if there were any—and stay away from baboons.

Behind him, Pirra coughed, and clawed at her dust-caked hair. "How much water's left?"

Hylas hefted the waterskin, then set it down again at the mouth of the cave. "Enough for a day. Maybe two."

She took that in silence, running her tongue over her chapped lips.

"We'll rest for a bit," he said, "but we can't sleep here all night."

"Why not?"

"The Sun, Pirra. We made a mistake, walking in daylight. From now on, we'll have to move by night, or we'll burn up."

"And go where?" she mumbled. "West again, and hope we can sneak past those baboons? Or keep going east, and pray that the river's this way?"

Hylas didn't answer. Neither sounded like much of a plan.

Taking what was left of the snake from his belt, he chucked it to her. "I'll go and gather some of that scrub and wake up a fire."

She glanced at the mangled carcass. "I'm not hungry."

"We need to eat. It'll taste better cooked."

The Sun was a bloody ball of fire sinking toward the horizon, but the heat was still crushing. As Hylas picked his way down the rocks, the ridge before him danced in the heat, and behind him, his shadow, stretching over the stones, was weirdly misshapen.

"What happens if we don't find anything," called Pirra. "Just more and more desert?"

"I don't know," he replied.

Out of the corner of his eye, he saw his shadow take on a life of its own.

It took Hylas a moment to realize that it wasn't his shadow, it was a boy, as dark as a shadow.

But by then the boy had snatched the waterskin and fled.

# THE
# GODS AND WARRIORS
# SERIES

## AND LOOK FOR THE FINAL BOOK
## IN THE SERIES, COMING SOON!